NOV. 2 4. 1987	DATE DUE	
DEC. 1 5. 1987		
MAY 1 7		
OCT 7 1989		
FEB 2 6 1990		
JUN 7 1990		
JUL 0 7 1995		

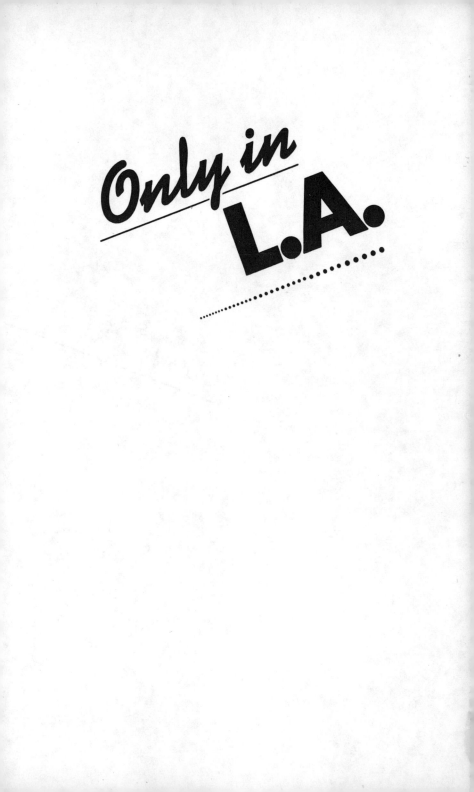

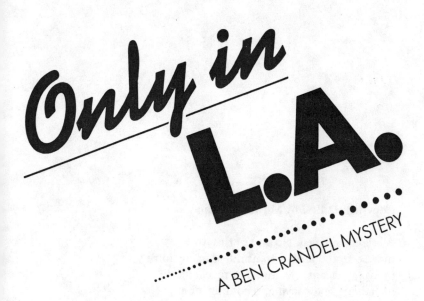

Only in L.A.

A BEN CRANDEL MYSTERY

MURRAY SINCLAIR

A&W Publishers NEW YORK

Published by
A & W Publishers, Inc.
95 Madison Avenue
New York, NY 10016

Manufactured in the United States of America
Designed by Levavi & Levavi

1 2 3 4 5 6 7 8 9 10

Library of Congress Cataloging in Publication Data

Sinclair, Murray.
  Only in L.A.
  I. Title.
PS3569.I52505   813'.54   81-70462
ISBN 0-89479-106-0   AACR

for Shelly Lowenkopf
& Patrick O'Connor

& Tootsie, always

"Hollywood is probably the most important and the most difficult subject for our time to deal with."

JOHN DOS PASSOS

1

It was one of those days I should have stayed home in bed—Lincoln's birthday—the day I got a singing telegram that was meant for someone else. It didn't do me any good. I was standing at my office window in one of the Producers' buildings at Burbank Studios, trying to daydream my way out of a boring rewrite, when a shrill voice broke into song just behind my back.

"Mister Shapiro, be a hero!"

I jumped, banging my forehead against the glass, then turned to greet my unexpected guest. She was a tall young blonde with a long flushed face, pointed chin, and large innocent gray eyes. Her best feature was her legs. They were long and well showcased. She seemed to be rigged up in a female counterpart to a hotel bellhop's uniform. Double rows of brass buttons lumped out from the thick navy blue flannel squashing down her chest. Beneath that, her narrow hips were banded by a short miniskirt of the same material. Her stockings were black and seamed and her shoes were relatively flat. A tiny red pillbox was fastened with bobbypins at a ludicrous angle on the top of her head.

Without intending it, I found myself sounding like an indignant gentleman. "What's the meaning of this?" I demanded.

The girl had stopped bleating. One leg was straight, the other bent with the metal tapped heel up off the carpet. She'd been soft-shoeing it to whatever she'd been belting out. Now she was frozen in the middle of her *schtick*. She put a hand behind her back, reached into the waistband of her short skirt, and came up with a wrinkled sheet of paper. She brought it close to her face, frowned, squinted, then looked up at me.

"Robert Shapiro?"

"No."

"This is Producers One, office one-oh-seven?"

"And his name's even on the door. But Mister Shapiro is not here."

"Jeeze," she sighed. "Is he coming back?"

"You mean you wanna do that bit all over again?"

Her flushed cheeks reddened. Her lips pursed. The end result was a 'Let's get on with it' smirk.

"He moved his office," I said bluntly. She started to open her mouth to ask where. I stopped her, adding, "No, I don't know where, can't think of whom you might ask, and don't care."

She straightened, putting her hands on her hips. Her chin came forward and her gray eyes turned a darker shade. "Listen," she said sternly. "I didn't mean to startle you, but it's not the end of the world, is it?"

I could have strangled her, so instead I enveloped my-

2

self in a shield of magnanimity and smiled at the situation.

"Of course not," I chuckled. "Now, Mister Shapiro's a casting director, isn't he? And you must have been sent by someone—an agent possibly—to remind him not to forget about a certain special so-and-so?"

The girl looked at her paper. "Susan Grady."

"She must be up for a pilot," I said sweetly.

"Something like that," mused the messenger.

"And who's the agent?"

She looked at her paper. "R. Baskin?"

"That's a big one," I smiled. "They're certainly industrious these days, aren't they?"

The girl knitted her brows, but somehow managed a smile. I was confusing her.

I smiled ear-to-ear. "What they won't think of next."

She started backing toward the door. "I better go see if I can find him," she said.

I made a stopping gesture with a raised forefinger. "One word of advice: next time, just a knock or two and make sure you've got the right party before you go into your routine—I mean, you don't want to waste yourself and get tired out."

"Yeah," she nodded.

"Well, bye now," I waved. I turned and walked back toward my desk. "And please *do* close the door."

I sat at my desk and got bored again. Susan Grady—I'd heard of her. She was a good actress. I'd seen her in a few local plays, then she'd had a big part in a long miniseries. A damn good actress, but pranks like this were destined to mummify her in tinsel. Singing telegrams—what could be tackier?

3

2

I couldn't work, so I got up and went into the outer office and came back with the West L.A. and Hollywood telephone directories. I spent the next half hour calling S. Gradys out of the phone book. Finally, I got the right one.

I wasn't sure, but I thought I recognized her voice. Low and throaty, a cross between Lauren Bacall and Brenda Vaccaro. My skin tingled, I got goose bumps. I couldn't exactly remember her looks, but her phone voice conjured a beautiful outline: tall, lithesome, reddish hair, and deliciously pale.

In short, after complimenting her on her work, I told her the whole incident and asked if she'd had any inkling that her agent was promoting her in such an asinine fashion. She hadn't and she agreed with me in thinking it strictly amateur-time.

"Pardon me for sounding precious," I told her, "but, as I said, I've admired your work, I remembered who you were, I think you have talent and—"

"I'm blushing," she intoned huskily.

I put my feet up on the desk, leaned back in my padded swivel chair, and stared dreamily up at my bullseye on the ceiling as I doodled over my scene outline without looking. "I can almost see it," I told her. "You're pretty, too, which doesn't hurt."

She said nothing in reply.

My heart sank. My pulse started racing. I realized that this whole conversation sounded like a deliberate scheming ploy. "I'm sorry," I said. "That has nothing to do with it."

She laughed. The side of my mouth twitched. I was Bogie again.

"Anyway, Susan," I went on, "as I said, I thought of you when the telegram arrived; and, as you seem to merit more than being packaged as today's hot-plate special, I thought I'd give a call."

"I don't know what to say."

"Just have a talk with your agent."

"Yeah, you're right."

"Of course I am." I loved myself. The studios were really rubbing off on me. I felt like executive material.

"Well . . ." she said awkwardly.

"Well is right," I mimicked.

"Maybe we should have a drink."

"Why, Susan, that's not why I called. . . but I'd like to. . . very much."

She laughed at me. "Oh, you're smooth."

"I went to finishing school."

"I'm gonna be busy this week. Call me, say Monday."

"Say Monday."

" 'Bye."

I sighed deeply and hung up humming the first few

bars of "The Girl from Ipanema." Someone coughed. I sat up as Samantha Kovac glided through the doorway, rolling her nice hips in a mock bossa nova. Her mouth was solemn, but her dark eyes glistened with laughter and mischief.

" 'How can I tell her I love her?' " she sang.

"You were listening!"

" 'Yes, I would give my heart gladly.' " Sam intertwined her fingers and made a heartbeat, bumpity-bump sign over her chest.

I laughed, but I was angry too. "You had no right," I said, trying for seriousness.

She came around the desk and plopped down sideways on my lap, hanging her arms around my neck and snuggling her bottom down at my groin. She pecked my cheek and laughed at me with her eyes. "Don't be guilty, darling. You're entitled to flirt. I do."

"We were making plans for a secret rendezvous."

"Ooo. I'm wet already. Could I watch?"

A direct hit. I leaned away, absorbing the blow. "You're serious, aren't you?"

"Oh, Ben." She patted my cheek in a motherly way.

"Well, goddamn it, Sam. Can't I make you jealous?"

"Benjy, so cute when he pouts."

I tried to smirk. My smirk failed me.

"You're so testy today," Sam frowned. She put a blood red forenail on the tip of her chin and pretended to be deep in thought for a moment. "I better take you out of town," she decided.

"Oh, really. But what about my other engagement?"

"That's Monday."

I pinched her nose. "That's why you're the boss, I suppose. You know everything."

And she did. Certainly enough to keep an upper hand on me. Sam was short, dark, thin, and slinky—a big little firecracker who threw her curves at you in a blasé way guaranteed to drive you crazy. It was hard to be close to her without trying to paw all her clothes off. At first, I'd fought the impulse. She was the company VP and head of Development. But she gave me the green light by the end of our first story conference and we'd been going hot and heavy ever since, over a month now, which, according to the L.A. exchange rate in relationships, has to be the equivalent of at least a year or two.

She was in green today, a gaudy emerald, and her skimpy dress had ridden halfway up her thighs. She got up and smoothed it out. Then she opened her small dull black leather handbag, took out a case of green Shermans, extracted one and lit up with a thin gold cylinder. She closed her eyes, tilted her head back, and blew a smoke ring.

I smiled and asked her to marry me, something I was in the habit of doing at least once a day.

"Maybe tomorrow when we're all grown up."

It was either that or "I'd better check my chart" or the converse of the first, "Aren't we a little old for that?" Still, even through the joking, there was an awkwardness that neither of us was able to understand. Underneath it all, I think we both wondered whether it could happen. You did what you wanted, when you wanted, for as long as you wanted—while presuming that somehow, in the end, the relationship would either sustain itself and exert its exclusivity or simply dry up, disappear. I guess it was tacitly assumed that, if it was going to happen, we'd end up hitched in the grand old manner for not having denied each other our various whims and pleasures. We were purists of a sort.

"Let's get serious," she was saying.

I took her hand. "Darling, I've been waiting to hear that."

She coughed, choking on her smoke as she laughed. "Not that, honey. I'm taking you off this script."

"What? I'm almost finished!"

"You can pick it up later. We want you to do something more important."

"I'll have to talk to my agent."

"Do. I already have. He's got nothing else lined up and has no qualms at all with you taking on another polish at three times what we paid you for this one."

The breath whistled through my lips. "That's a lot of dough."

"Stick with me, kid. I told our legals to draft the contract, but if you don't mind, dear, we'd like to get on this right away."

"What is it?"

"A feature with Alfie Wilde."

"You're kidding. He does all his own stuff. What do you need me for?"

"Shades of yesteryear, dear. I know he's one of your camp favorites, but even the great grow old and, well, Alfie's had a little crack-up."

"You're kidding."

"Stop the gee-whiz, Benjy. Want a lollipop?"

"But he's great. He's one of my idols."

"Forget that. Listen: it's another one of his aging-screen-siren epics. Alfie gave us his first draft—not awful but it needs lots of work."

"He's used to that. After all, I know there were at least twenty on *Lost Star*."

"Great film, but his erstwhile collaborator's dead and Alfie's gone bonkers. He was on the wagon for fifteen years, now suddenly he's off."

"Is he still married to that what's-her-name?"

"Madeline Christy. Sure. Nothing explains it."

The company president, old Bernard Marks, was also

one of the writer-director's best friends. According to
Sam, no one had the slightest idea. Presently, Wilde was
drying out in a posh Westwood sanitarium. The more
we hashed it around, the real issue that surfaced seemed
to be one of taking the script away from the old master
while somehow managing to stay in his good graces. The
company needed his name attached to the project and,
besides, he was co-producer which meant that one to
two million of his hardearned nuggets were in the kitty,
with the start date on production virtually hours away.
Alfie didn't know it but they had already hired another
director. And since I was one of the man's biggest fans,
they thought it might work if I were the one to drop all
their turds.

3

It was a nasty mess. I put on my corduroy jacket and Sam walked me across the lot to her executive office in the Columbia Towers. Stepping out of the Producers' building, we hit the plain back of New York Street. From this side, it was the rear view of an old grandstand that had seen better days. At the far end, there was a small sign: Fantasy Island Wardrobe. Next to it, a trailer wedged along the wall looked like it was standing vigil to keep the whole pile from crumbling down upon our heads. You passed more trailers going by the tottering rubble of Tenement Street where a high draft fingered the shredded curtains in the top story by the fire escape. I was gripped by nostalgia as I imagined how the great Alfie must have felt, having unfettered command of the monolith when it was new and fresh to the touch and things that could never happen again happened, then, for the first time. Everything that went on here now was a tired restatement, a hashing over. What in the world could possibly compare with *The Jazz Singer,* the first sound film, and that startling array of the best tough-guy talkies ever made, than the stylish flair of Alfie's profound talent. Subtly, he had perfected the form. He tore his stories straight out of the daily headlines, then stirred them with his genius. I got goose bumps just thinking of the man. When it came to films, in my league Alfie owned them; and Sam, though I loved her, and these other cretins had the temerity to think they could pull the wool over his eyes. Well, it couldn't be done, and it wouldn't—not by me.

We came into the Towers, passed the security man, and took the elevator up to Sam's office on the top floor. She handed me a Coors along with five sheets of single-spaced type and sat beside me on the couch.

I looked at the first page: "Alfie Wilde Project—Synopsis by B. Roth." "I don't like it," I told her.

She poured hers into a narrow-stemmed glass, sipped it and licked the foam moustache off her upper lip while winking at me with a naughty look. I must have frowned. She started using my last name.

"Crandel, Crandel," she sighed. "Think."

"I'm thinking. That's why I don't like it."

"You're a fan of Alfie's."

"That's putting it mildly."

"Let me finish," she said shortly. "You're a great admirer of Wilde's work. O.K. You think he deserves respect and decent treatment. O.K. But realize, if you don't take this on, somebody else will. More likely than not, they'll fail to handle him with the soft kid gloves you might have employed; ergo, end result equals one mortally wounded Alfie, one lost film for us. It's up to you,

Ben. You could help us all the way around and work with your idol to boot."

I drank the beer, finished it, then got up and found myself another. "As I see it, from what you mentioned crossing the yard, it's not really work, it's subterfuge or, more accurately, sabotage. You want me to take your reader's suggested list of revisions—" I flicked the paper. "And who the hell this guy is I don't know from Adam."

"Gal."

"What right does some kid—"

"She's thirty-one years old. She's been involved in a number of major projects."

"I don't care who the hell she is or what she's done. You have no right to tear apart a Wilde first draft. That's for Wilde. He's the only one who can do it."

"But, as I told you, he can't right now."

"Then hold off the picture."

"That, I'm afraid, is impossible."

"When you deal with a great man, you do so in good faith, with dignity."

My sentimentality tickled Sam with a smile, but she wiped it off quickly. "That's what you're going to do," she said mildly.

I took the five pages, crumpled them into a ball and squeezed it with both hands. "You want me to take this pill, digest it, and pretend to collaborate with Wilde while plugging in all these pre-programmed decisions. That's fucked."

"Then forget it."

Quickly, I thought over what she'd said. If I didn't take this thing, somebody else would and they might follow their orders to the letter. On the other hand, I could agree to terms, then talk turkey with Wilde and turn the tables on them.

"Fuck it. I'll take it," I said.

"On our terms," Sam said clearly.

Sabotage! "Sure."

"He'll probably agree to most of your or 'our' ideas anyway. Bernie's talked to him already and he's been quite sweet."

"You just don't want him to feel fucked over."

"It's a delicate situation," Sam smiled. "Something with Wilde's name, after all, we don't want it to come out being an embarrassment."

"True."

"And there's leeway." Sam pointed to the paper pill. "Just use that as a guideline."

"OK."

"But use it."

"OK, OK already."

"Can you get started this afternoon?"

"My kid's off school today. I'm taking him to the museum."

"How cultural."

"Exactly. He needs culture and I gotta make sure he gets it."

"Forced feeding?"

I finished off the second beer and squished the can. I didn't say anything.

Sam sat up straight and leaned forward, chin in hand. "Sorry."

"I know. . . . Tryin' to raise that young upstart up right . . ." I said, forcing a smile.

Sam was staring at me, waiting. Her secretary was out to lunch. I knew what she was thinking about, but as I leaned down and brushed her lips I already had too much on my mind.

4 ....

A couple of hours later, my kid, Petey, and I were coming out of the Los Angeles County Art Museum over by Wilshire and Fairfax. When it comes to art, you have to be very patient with L.A. There isn't usually too much to see unless the L.A. County or the Norton Simon decides to shake hands with itself and honor the collection of one of their huge benefactors with a special exhibit accompanied by a pretty color program and brief italicized bio covering the highlights of the collector's larger-than-life career: *B. S. Crudball, noted philanthropist and businessman, first came to Los Angeles in 1913 with three dead fleas and a piece of pumpernickel in his back pocket. He began pumping gas, then after years of sacrifice and loathsome hard work, he charted his course toward loftier goals, finally chairing the board of Lotsa*

Oil Corp. where he now makes like a tuba blowing through solid gold hemorrhoids into a velvet whoopee cushion whilst directing many destinies.

It's quite hard to fathom how these guys somehow mellow into attaining particular affinities for the French Rococo style, but nevertheless, regardless of motive, many of them do and they end up having pretty nifty collections. This guy had everything: Frangonards, Watteaus, Monets, Van Goghs, Renoirs, Eakins, Cassatts, Sargents, Picassos, and so much more, but I knew better than to expect my thirteen-year-old to get tripped out by it. "Forced feeding" Sam had said. Sure it is, but I'm not the type who makes a point of standing by the door with an hour glass to make sure my little darling gets in her daily practice on the ukulele. Just a little exposure, that's all. Then if they want more they'll seek it out themselves. In the meantime, at least they'll know it's there.

With my kid, you practically have to take him by the neck and put his nose up against the canvas just to get him to eyeball a few paintings. It's like paper training a puppy. We must have spent ten minutes inside and when we came out he looked cowed and sulky like I'd just lashed him with a barber strap. Damn. It's no picnic raising a kid. Especially when you've adopted him and known him for only three years and he's lived with you for only two of them and has nothing but bonafide blank spots when it comes to remembering his real folks and a lot of his past. And especially when you come from the same stock yourself. The kiddie courts, juvenile hall, foster homes, and orphanages of every denomination— both of us had been through it all. Who wants to remember it and why would you care to recall bad times and bad people?

The blind leading the blind. But at least I understand him. He knows that. He's always known it, ever since I started out as his Big Brother—three years ago and it seems like a century. He had grown about a foot since then and his freckles were vanishing. In their place, I'd noticed lately, he was growing body hair, little bristles under his arms and around his pubes. His skinny arms were getting muscular and I didn't have to yell at him to shower anymore; on the other hand, he wouldn't cut his hair. He had long thick dark blond ringlets down to his shoulders and spent an inordinate amount of time attending to them with the pocket comb he now seemed to have in his possession at all times. He concealed it well, but my suspicion was that he was starting to get actively interested in girls. My precious little J.D. was growing up. There was something just a touch sad about it. Petey was my baby boy, my flesh and blood like no other could possibly be. He was a carbon copy of me. I loved him firecely but we hadn't been talking too much as of late. He was getting too fucking tough to have anything to do with idle chatter. Voluntarily, he didn't share nothin' with me anymore. I was *The Law*, which was why I was having to come up with things for us to do together. The anger was starting to boil up in him. He didn't know what it was or exactly where it came from, but it was there. Sometimes, I thought he wanted me to be an ogre so he could hate me and have something concrete to focus his frustration on. Meanwhile, I was trying to break myself of the habit of spoiling him. Bribes postpone the rebellion, muffle the clashes. You don't want to fight with your own kid, so you spoil him rotten to make him feel guilty when he starts acting up. In the end, or along the way, it just makes him nastier and draws out the whole goddamn process.

Kids.

So we came outside and played around with his expensive Christmas present. I stood by the museum door and Petey walked across the patio, lighting up a Kool as his voice came over on the walkie-talkie.

"Read me? Over," he asked, sounding bored with his month-old toy.

I pressed the talk button. "Natch. Over."

"I'm hungry. Over."

"Good spies don't have time to worry about their bellies. Over."

"But there ain't nothin' ta spy on."

"Don't whine. You forgot your 'Over'. Over."

"Come on, Ben. Over."

"Where are we going? Over."

No answer.

"Petey, are you there? Over."

"Yeah."

"OK. I think I hear my stomach growling. Let's get Stanley. Over."

Petey turned around from the other end of the court, flicked away his cigarette, and came walking toward me. We met at the center staircase. I put my arm over his shoulder and we walked down to the sidewalk fronting Wilshire Boulevard where my basset hound, Stanley, was tied up around the leg of a pretzel cart. I bought us each a rope-thick pretzel, smeared some mustard on mine, and gave the high school kid a ten dollar bill. He started to make change.

"Keep it," I told him. "You're a superb sitter."

"Well, Stanley's quite a conversationalist," the kid beamed, looking up from a thick paperback entitled *Survey of Philosophy*.

"He thinks we live in a Hegelian universe."

The kid closed his book. Mischief glinted from behind his thick specs. "He did seem preoccupied with trying to grasp the essence of virtue as it correlates with social

conformity or the obedience to governmental authority."

Deep in thought, I rubbed my chin and looked down
at Stanley. His black, white, and tan mottled coat was
still clean and shiny from the bath I'd given him a few
days before. He was wagging his tail, but his sunken
bright eyes gazed above me, sadly supplicating the stern
silent heavens beyond, and his front feet were widely
splayed which gave his head and shoulders a drooping,
weightily burdened appearance. Yes, he seemed moved
by an injustice of an overwhelmingly metaphysical nature.

I looked back at the young pretzel vendor. "Perhaps
it's because he's tied up," I speculated.

"Let's give him some credit," the young man frowned.
"It's beyond that."

"Maybe you're right," I shrugged, bending down to lift
up a wheel of the stand and unhitch the leash.

I said "So long" and the three of us walked away. Petey
seemed to be brooding. He never likes it when he doesn't
understand what you're talking about.

"Philosophy," I said by way of explanation.

Petey shrugged and looked around. We were moving
east on Wilshire beside the large main La Brea Tar Pit.
On the west edge of the pit on a raised mound was a big
gray white cement replica of one of the extinct American
Mastodon fossils they'd found buried deep in the oily
gook.

"In a couple years, you may be interested in bullshit
like that," I was saying.

Without saying anything, Petey turned and looked at
me like I was crazy.

"You start wondering why you're here, what it all
means," I continued. "Then you get confused or too
busy and decide it doesn't matter."

"What the fuck are you talkin' about?" he barked with irritation.

"Forget it," I smiled. "Doesn't matter."

Stanley pulled me over to a lamp pole by the curb and Petey and I stood there and waited for the philosopher to relieve himself.

"Look over there."

Petey pointed toward the east end of the Tar Pit. I could see a mass of people grouped together on the top platform of the single story observation deck. Next to them, others were pressed up against the black cyclone fence encircling the pit. It seemed unlikely that the three cement Imperial Mammoths would be doing anything too spectacular down there. After all, the beasts themselves had been extinct a million and a half years and I doubted that the park service had recently acquired a Disneyland fortune to provide the lifesized models with locomotive powers.

At that point, a pair of squad cars galloping west turned sharp right at the corner before us, cranked up their sirens and killed them just as fast as they braked to a quick stop out of view.

Needless to say, it was *de rigueur* that we check it out. I let Petey go ahead. He ran back to the path that cuts through the park and around the pit before the George C. Page Rancho La Brea Museum. I followed behind with Stanley.

The benches on the grass, shaded by the scrubby little trees, were empty. All of the *alter kockers* from the Fairfax district had moved over to the east end of the pit. This had to be some event to warrant breaking up their daily *kibbitzing* and *shrying*. I let Stanley walk me along to a few more pit stops and by that time Petey was coming over on the walkie-talkie.

"Ben, Ben. Are you there? Over."

"Yeah. Over."

"Somebody's floatin' in the tar pit. Over."

"Nice place to take a dip. Probably a new wonder remedy for wrinkles and dry skin."

"It's a dead body, and that guy you know, Detective Steifer—"

"Captain, please," interrupted a much lower voice in a jocular tone. "Crandel, get your ass over here."

"Oh, Christ," I sighed into the walkie-talkie.

"No, George," came back. "Is your memory that short?"

"How the hell ya' doin'?" I asked, meanwhile looking up ahead for the two of them as Stanley and I rushed forward.

When I got over there, a half-dozen uniform cops were directing the foot traffic. They had gotten the folks off the observation deck and blocked the steps and were trying to keep the others away from the borders of the fence. Steifer looked unusually spiffy, all five feet five of him. I hadn't seen him in over a year. His jet black hair was combed dry and styled without a part. He was wearing a tweedy light brown suit with narrow lapels and a thin royal blue tie. I'd had some trouble with this man a while back. After the trouble was over, I'd called him to say hello and apologize for having been difficult and we'd become fair weather friends—a relationship I'd define by saying that we'd had a couple drinks and played poker together once or twice. I'd played in his game with his overjolly cop buddies and he'd played in my circus of coke crazy writers and actors. Neither of us had felt too comfortable out of our natural habitats and, like foreign pen pals, we had stopped communing for lack of anything new or interesting to say. But Steifer was an all-right guy. I used to think of him as Ferret face. If he didn't trust you, the little man used every ounce of his small sinewy overworked muscle to sniff out every dirty dream you'd ever had. He could radiate an uncompromising, near insane meanness if he so chose; on the flip side, if he decided he liked you, he tended to be mild, like an awkward shy boy, and wanted to know your birthday so he could be sure to send you a card.

The uniformed boys tried to stop my progress, but Steifer gave them a short curt whistle and they looked over the shoulder, then nodded me through. I sauntered over and made fun of Steifer's dry look by fingering his coat shoulder and nodding with thoughtful approval.

"Nice. So how they hangin'?" I asked him.

Steifer looked a little embarrassed. He rolled his eyes and shook his head for the benefit of his young wooden partner. Then he stuck out his small hand and rotated his wrist, flipping the palm up and down. "*Comme ci, comme ca,*" he grinned.

"That's what *she* said," I grinned back.

"Crandel, Crandel. Always the wise ass."

"I'm just celebrating seeing you without being a suspect."

Steifer shrugged his shoulder in the direction of the other plainclothes. "Bob Armstead," he said.

Armstead and I shook hands, but Stanley broke the ice with him by sticking his nose in the guy's pant cuff. He cracked a smile and bent down for a pat. "Nice dog," he said.

Stanley licked Armstead over the nose and glasses. He made a face and stood up, taking off his specs and going over them with a hanky. There was a thin white line of scar tissue slanting down over his left eyebrow. I noticed it because it seemed so unlikely on him. Otherwise, the guy looked like a worried young executive who had just misplaced his briefcase.

"Remember me?" Steifer asked Petey.

"Sure," Petey nodded. "We had our picture taken together."

Petey hardly needed to be reminded. My old girlfriend Ellen had done a magazine piece on my run-in with Steifer and all the other events that had preceded and followed. Good and bad people had lost their lives and, in the aftermath, Petey had lost another candidate for mother. There had been others since, but Ellen had been the first near miss. My hunch was it still hurt him.

"That's right." Steifer put a paw over Petey's shoulder and massaged it. "You're gettin' big, kid. Wanna fight?"

"Better watch out," I warned. "He's got a mean right cross."

Steifer made the kid show it and eventually got Petey's solid small fist in his middle and didn't seem to have a hard time pretending it hurt. We were waiting for the museum curator to return with a dinghy so they could go out into the pit. An orchid-colored meat wagon from the coroner's office came around the corner at a leisurely pace. In a few moments, it was coming toward us over the park grass. A few patrolmen detached themselves from the crowd detail and stepped toward the van, waving it forward. It came up to us, then backed up and turned around so that the twin rear doors faced closest to the padlocked fence gate. The driver and the assistant coroner stepped out from the front. A husky guy came out through the rear doors. The man in charge wore a tan gabardine three piece that bulged over his ample middle. The other guys had white coats on over street-clothes and wore their shirts open at the collar. The husky one was wearing jogging shoes.

Steifer pointed at the corpse. All you could see of it was a dark foot and a raised white mound that seemed to be a bloated belly.

I didn't understand what Steifer was doing there. We were in West Hollywood territory and I thought he was Beverly Hills. It turned out he'd left Beverly Hills for what he called "political reasons" and he was back in West Hollywood where he said he'd been originally, making more money and pulling rank. He was in the running for Deputy Chief, his partner chipped in proudly, but Steifer simply smiled spacily and didn't seem to care. He appeared to have a lot on his mind and, without talking about it, I suspected that something had happened between him and his wife. If he didn't bring it up, it was none of my business. Besides, I might be wrong.

"Know anything about this?" I asked him.

"The museum guard called half an hour ago and said people were staring at a foot in the pit. So we came over. All we know's there's a body out there. *You* wouldn't happen to know anything, would you?"

"Don't start with me," I smirked.

The coroner interrupted us. Steifer explained the situation to him and he went back to his truck. Steifer turned back to Armstead and took up where he'd left off. "Crandel here's a little like fly paper or ant poison. Put him out there and things come to him and stick."

I shook my head. "Here we go again."

Steifer laughed and squinted as he tried to meet my eyes through my shades. "I mean, just the fact you're here, Crandel. I suppose that's gotta tell us something.'

"Shit," I said.

"Accessory after the fact?" Armstead smiled knowingly, joining the fun.

"Yeah. Maybe it goes deeper, though," Steifer mused, rubbing his chin. Petey whispered something in Steifer's ear.

"Kid says you confessed in your sleep," the cop smiled.

I smiled lovingly at my progeny and whacked him on the arm in kind. I turned back to Steifer, asking, "But how do you even know it's a murder?"

"Hmmm . . . good point," Steifer said to himself, then turned to Armstead. "He has a way with procedure, hasn't he?"

Armstead nodded and asked me if I'd ever been through the academy or studied criminology. No, I said, it came naturally.

Yep. The Coroner, his boys, the cops, and the crowd of old people and tourists were all waiting for the body to come out, and there we were shooting the breeze like a squadron of swallows whooping it up on our way back to Capistrano. Looking back on it now, it seems like every bit of this period of time, starting with that fucking singing telegram—it just seems like everything happened in slow motion. I can remember all of it, how people looked, what they said, and every goddamn little thing that happened. These few days, though I didn't realize it then, brought about a chain of events that I can liken only to a guillotine. Soon, I would have my head chopped off and after that I'd have to run about trying to find it. I can safely say I've never been more miserable. What could a dead unseen body in a scummy black pond have to do with me? For the moment, nothing. In hours, it would be everything.

5 . . . .

"**E**xcuse me. Vould you be the officer in charge?"

Steifer turned around. It was an old Jewish lady with fleecy snow white hair and thick tinted glasses that gave her gray eyes that underwater look. She wore a knee length dress of blue and white seersucker with a heavy white sweater buttoned to the neck. She was holding the B'nai B'rith *Messenger* and a Yiddish newspaper in one hand, with a small bag bulging over the top with fat succulent-looking oranges in the other.

"Yes. May I help you?"

"They told me that I should see you if I have some information," the old lady said carefully.

Steifer nodded.

"I was the one that was first with the spotting of that foot," she said, pointing toward the half-submerged corpse. She pulled up her sleeve, revealing a cheap Timex above her liver-spotted hand, tapped the crystal with a short pink nail. "The time was exactly one-forty-five," she said. "One and a quarter hours ago. Exactly. Someone I am with can be a witness, but they went home upset."

"Thank you very much." Steifer bent down a little and met the nice old lady's eye. "I appreciate your telling me."

"You vant my name perhaps?"

"I don't think that will be necessary."

"Vell, I hope this is taken care of," she sighed sadly.

"Me too," Steifer smiled.

"Here. You have an orange."

Steifer shook his head no. "Thanks," he said.

She turned to me. "You?"

"I'm not a policeman," I confessed.

"That's all right," she nodded solemnly.

I hesitated.

She put her newspaper hand under the bag and lifted it toward my face. "*Essen,*" she urged me.

I took one. She made a silent motion that I should talk to Steifer, then she turned and walked away. Petey and I split the orange. It tasted even better than it looked. I watched the old woman as she walked around the side-walk bordering the pit and rejoined a group of nine or ten old people who were standing by the fence across the way from the body. A few of them came toward her. They were all jabbering and she yelled something, then put her bag and newspapers down on a bench and started gesturing with both hands as she proudly told them her story.

After everybody started looking around and checking their watches, two men came toward us carrying a bat-tered eight-foot aluminum rowboat. One of them had a wispy blond beard and short bowl-cut hair. He wore dirty jeans and a flannel shirt with hiking boots. The other was wearing a knee-length white coat over an ugly plain brown suit. His open-necked white shirt was spotted with oil and clay and his tanned forehead was narrow and domey with a full head of graying brown hair pulled straight back and tied at the back into a braided ponytail that disappeared under the lab jacket. His eyes were a little on the glassy side; his lips carried an ever-present beatific smile. He looked happy-go-lucky in the holier-than-thou sixties fashion.

They set down their dinghy and the one in the long white coat stepped forward. His fingernails shone black from the constant close work with oil and asphalt in unearthing and scraping clean the endless bounty of ancient bones.

Steifer nodded to both of us. "Doctor Backer, Ben Crandel."

We performed our 'pleased to meet you's,' then Dr. Backer unlocked the gate and started through with his assistant. The Deputy Coroner stopped him, saying that he'd have to handle it, then he ordered his boys into the boat and the rest of us stood there and watched the tar bubble up around the shore of the pit. Infrequently, from farther out, a large bubble or two surfaced from what appeared to be the depths.

"How deep is this thing?" Petey asked the doc.

"Funny you should ask," he said. "What would you guess?"

"I came here with somebody once who said it was bottomless," Petey told him. "It's gotta be pretty deep, doesn't it?"

Backer smiled broadly, shaking his head. "This spot has a mythic reputation. We've had mental patients, old men, and distraught actresses climb the fence and try to make the plunge. All they do is sprain their necks."

Petey frowned at the big words, then repeated his question.

"If you jumped in right now—and the pond's at its deepest at this time of year—you'd have a pretty hard time swimming without scraping your knees and elbows. There's approximately three feet of water here over a bed of three feet of tar. Most of that tar now is solid. It isn't hot for long enough now for the tar to heat up. That's how it got the animals. They could come and drink here during the winter, but when it got hot for a short while, they'd come and sink in with their great weight and get caught."

I looked at the water. It still looked fathomless, but now I realized that it was the black tar bottom that gave the illusion of such great depth.

Backer was staring out at the deputy coroner's boys who were prodding at the corpse with a ten foot rubber tipped pole they'd taken from the van and assembled in two pieces.

The deputy coroner cupped his hands over his fleshy jowls and yelled at his assistants: "Careful for bruising!" When his hands came away, his pale round face had reddened. His vest tightened as he blew out a big breath.

Backer gave a short laugh and shook his head some more. "It's a mess to get them out of there if they don't want to come."

The guys in the boat weren't getting anywhere. They stopped prodding the corpse and rowed over to it. The husky boy took the metal prod apart and handed half to the other guy. They worked on the body from the middle, securing the pole in the gook underneath and using that and the mass of the corpse as a fulcrum as they leaned their weight on the pole ends and pushed downwards. The Deputy Coroner cupped his hands and yelled again. He looked like this over-exertion was pushing him toward a coronary. The guys in the boat stopped their prodding from the north side and went around to the south where they did the same thing. I could hear the huskier one grunting from where I was standing. Backer explained that the body had started sinking into the tar. Considering the shallow depth, his guess was that it had only been there a short period of time.

At that point, the corpse's round belly rose a bit, then disappeared. The Coroner's assistants had pried the body loose and flipped it over onto its stomach. After that, they leaned over the water and scooped him up. The slighter guy had hold of something and lost it. The husky guy yelled, then picked up the body by himself. The other guy sat with his arms crossed and watched as the husky fellow hefted the body and laid it out face up over the boat sides. Calves and feet hung over one side, head and shoulders the other. It had short hair.

Everyone got quiet. All you could hear were the cars on Wilshire and the sound of the husky guy paddling toward us from the middle of the pond. He cut through the weedy oily scum and came up to the shore on the southeast edge. Dr. Backer went over to meet him with his assistant. The rest of us stayed where we were. The husky fellow put the pole together and handed it across to Backer while securing his end between his knees and holding it with both hands. Backer pulled the boat around the shore toward the gate until it snagged, coming aground. The husky guy stood up and, without saying anything, cocked his right hand and slugged the other guy in the arm.

"Fuck off," said the slighter guy.

The husky guy laughed, showing missing teeth, then the slight guy joined him. They lifted the body off the boat. The slight guy moved down toward the feet and grabbed onto the body by the ankles, while the husky guy hoisted from under the shoulders. The corpse's head dropped backward and bobbed back and forth with their movements.

They approached us. It was a little old man. A thin fringe of dirty white hair was plastered to his skull. Like a piece of putty, the face was spreading out, being pulled flat. The lips had swollen into a leering pout and the fleshiness of the nose seemed to have broadened. All of it was covered with a dark, brackish residue which showed white on the side of one cheek from where it had been scraped clean by the coroner boys' meddling. A combination of oil and sludge had formed deposits in the eye cavities. He wore black pants with matching support hose and a white shirt that had turned the color of dish water. All of him was puffy, but his stomach was grotesque. His right hand was black with oil; on the same hand, the cuff was open and the sleeve hung from his elbow, showing a bluish white forearm.

Stanley was sniffing like crazy. He'd be motionless for a moment, then he'd tug at the leash and start moving toward the body with a little howling whine. Petey looked a little pale.

Armstead pulled nervously at an ear lobe as he walked ahead and leaned over the corpse. Coming back to us, he leaned toward Steifer, saying, "A question we gotta ask right away, I think—"

Steifer held a hand up as he interrupted in a hushed voice. "How did such an old man climb the fence to get in there?"

"Exactly," the younger man nodded.

Steifer looked around, using his dark eyes to gesture at the crowd. "Look at these old people, Armstead. They're upset. Number one, they're upset because they're old and there's nothing they can do about it. Two, their children never do the right thing by them—

nothing they can do about that either. Three, they're made helpless by world events, namely the plight of Israel and urban blight, white flight, and crime. They've got this park where they can come and sit and complain about all of it and we don't want to scare the shit out of them and ruin that too, do we?"

Armstead grimaced and shook his head from side to side. He knew he'd done wrong.

"So, let's save the investigation till we get back to the office, shall we?"

"Sure, George," Armstead smiled sheepishly.

Petey was staring toward the coroner's wagon. "Jesus," he sighed.

I turned to him and rubbed a hand into his shoulder. "We're going," I said.

Steifer gave the kid a pat on the head and we told each other we'd give a call with that well meant sincerity you use when you really want to but know you're never going to get around to it.

I didn't know it, but I'd be seeing him sooner than I thought.

6

We didn't get to Pink's until four o'clock. Petey had been quiet all day, but seeing that waterlogged old man had set him brooding. I knew I should have dragged him away from there before they got the body out, but with bumping into Steifer and all the ensuing commotion, I'd let us dillydally around longer than I'd intended. But I didn't want to shelter the kid either. He had to know about life and death and what can happen to you and he certainly wasn't going to get a very realistic picture on TV. Still, it was a shock.

I asked the counterman for extra chili and got us two dogs apiece along with orange soda and a plain dog for Stanley. The chili was thick and sweet, the dogs were boiled plump, the buns just delivered. Perfect. After that, the kid's glumness lifted somewhat. We crossed the

street to the MG and took La Brea straight up to Hollywood Boulevard, turned right, caught the Hollywood
Freeway over at Highland Avenue, took it straight to
Lankershim and headed on south to Nudie's. Nudie, an
eighty year old Russian immigrant, tools around in a
$150,000 white Cadillac convertible with a set of big bull
horns protruding from the front grill, and runs the flash-
iest custom western-wear shop in existence. Elvis used
to have his $10,000 gold lamé suits made there. Cher
has him sew rhinestones in her navel. Even Nudie's
stock apparel is fit to knock your eyes out and I'd prom-
ised Petey a shirt as fair payment for the museum excur-
sion, so that's why we were there.

Stanley and I tried on a couple of ten gallon hats and
stared at a lifelike watercolor of lifeless John Wayne,
photos of Elvis, Marilyn, Gable, Alan Ladd, and Audie
Murphy in a display case set off by a banner stating,
"Their Last Curtain." I got tired of that, took Petey by
the elbow, and straggled toward Nudie's office in the
back. No one was in there. We gawked at the inscribed
stripper pictures on the walls, then moved back into the
main showroom. Petey finally picked out a light blue
gabardine number trimmed with black on the cuffs,
yoke, and pockets, and put it on over his T-shirt. I paid
old Mrs. Nudie and we headed on home to Laurel Canyon.

I called Sam out at Burbank and got the address of
Alfie Wilde's sanitarium. He was expecting me. I was
supposed to meet Sam at her house when I was done
and then we were going to drive up to Santa Barbara for
the night and have the whole next day to frolic on the
beach at the Biltmore, that is, if this strange late Indian
summer lasted long enough. The sky had started cloud-
ing up around an hour ago. We were due for rain.

I told the kid I'd be away for the night and, of course,

he didn't seem to mind. I suggested he have one of his friends over—that way he'd stay up all night in the house instead of running around in the street. I made it very clear that he was to be in by ten and then he took the phone into the bathroom to call his friend. A history professor with a weakness for poker and horses lived in a studio apartment above the cleaners down at the base of the hill by Cafe Galleria and the Country Store. I walked down to his place to ask him to look in on Petey, and came back to the kid and unveiled the insurance backing up my curfew threat. He did not look pleased. He turned on the TV and lit up a Kool, coughing on the first puff.

I laughed and left the house, taking Laurel all the way down to Olympic Boulevard, then proceeding west out past Sawtelle and turning up a couple of blocks north. I was there before I'd had time to think about it. The place was called *The Westside*. Two small identifying cement plaques were set at ground level on either side of a short walk bordered by tall untrimmed cypresses that swept down from the entrance, then angled out around the entire corner lot. Being stuck smack dab in the middle of a lower middle class neighborhood, they probably wanted it that way for the seclusion. You couldn't even see the building. Across the street, beat up old heaps, rusty tricycles, and a discarded stove were parked over a few of the front lawns. A candy-lacquered low rider was on display in one of the driveways.

The door was one of those machine-carved relief jobs that someone imaginative might have called Spanish Mediterranean. I tried to open it, but it wouldn't budge. A battered speakbox centered the pebbly white right sidewall.

I pushed the button. "Hello? Ben Crandel to see Alfie Wilde."

No answer. I repeated my calling card two more times,

then I just stood there and leaned against the wall. I was making up my mind to look around for another entrance when the door swung open and a guy around my age and height came bouncing out. His arms swung loosely by his sides in long front-to-back arcs. He looked sideways at me, blinked a pair of over-brilliant pale blue eyes, and broke into a childish giggle as he loped on down the cypress-lined walk at a tilted, off-balance gait, moving like a six-foot human wind up doll. He was barefoot in faded Levi's and a white T-shirt with red handwritten lettering that said *Heaven*. His wavy hair was on end and pressed flat in the back like he'd just woken up from a nap. I caught the door and went in as he started singing "The hills are alive with the sound of music" at the top of his lungs.

I was just inside the door, standing by a tightly packed cluster of three unoccupied desks in the dimly lit reception area, chuckling to myself over what I'd just seen and heard, when Karem Abdul Jabar's brother glided in from an open doorway on the left. He shook his long black face at me from two stories above, then pursed his thick lips with a mildly chastising expression. He wore a collarless white tunic with side buttons at the neck over tight dark slacks. His pocket nameplate said *Everett Watson*.

"Tsk, tsk," he said without moving his lips.

"I'm here to—" I started to say.

Everett put his hands on his hips and scowled at me like Muhammad Ali used to while he was making up his mind how and when he was going to whup you. "Don't give me that shit," he said calmly, the pursed lips spreading into a little smile. "Want your dinna, sucka?"

"Whoa, Ev. Wait a minute. He went thata way." I pointed toward the door. "I'm here to visit somebody."

It's strange how they look at you when they think you're crazy. It's enough to convince you that you are.

Everett had me by the arm as a bullish woman in her late fifties sashayed toward us from the hall dabbing at her clear dry eyes with a Kleenex. She wore a sheer pink evening dress that had been tailor-made for Ann-Margret; unfortunately, it was on the wrong body. Her charm bracelets jingle-jangled and she was wearing a teardrop diamond pendant that looked heavy enough to break its gold chain. She glanced at us and turned toward the door.

"Found him," Ev told her with his deep voice.

She whipped around with her chin high. Her round face had too much blush on it. She looked like she was plugged into an electric current. "What?!" Her voice came harsh and nasal. She seemed to be feigning that she had no idea how she'd got here. I would have thought she was an inmate if she hadn't been so gussied up.

Ev crushed my shoulders between his huge palms and pushed me forward.

"Oh, really, that's hardly him. Is this how you run this —hospital? I can't quite believe it."

Either could I. The lady sounded like she was having words with her waiter over a cold piece of meat. "He walked out as I came in," I offered.

Her brows knit as she glowered at me, then turned back to Ev. "Well," she said.

Ev let go of me and stood there looking bored.

"Aren't you going to find him?" she demanded. "Or do I have to?"

Ev's mouth tightened. His left cheek folded into a wrinkled little twitch. He crossed his arms over his stomach.

"Nobody knows what they're doing around here," she sneered, tilting her chin at the tall man's stomach. That's why *he's* like that."

She disappeared down the hall. I told the guy I was looking for Alfie Wilde. He laughed a little and apologized as he escorted me in the same direction. Mommy's high heels click-clacked along the linoleum and her wide flat buttocks joggled about, out of control, like a platter of disturbed jello. A nursing station was up ahead. We passed it as she stopped to talk to an Oriental woman in white who was sitting on a high stool at a counter-top desk behind three walls of glass.

"I'll be out, but I want that message left as soon as you find him."

She really cared. You wonder why some people even bother going through the motions. Ev and I shook our heads as we walked by the central rec room where residents and guests were focused on a black and white early show that had something to do with bombs over Tokyo. We turned down a short side corridor and walked toward the open exit at the end. A group was playing volleyball on a small court just outside the door. The white ball stood out in the dusk. Open palms made halfhearted slaps and pats against it until a tall silhouette forgot about the teamwork lesson and fisted it out of view. Voices grumbled, someone shouted, and a whistle trilled like a randy lovebird.

Ev knocked on the closed door beside the exit. Somebody yelled something indistinguishable, which my black guide took as an open invitation to march right in. He swung the door open and we entered the small dark room. A freshly made single bed faced the door from the far left corner. A small card table with two metal folding chairs was in the center. Cards were everywhere. Part of a solitaire hand was on the card table and the rest of it had been swept onto the floor. On the nightstand by the bed, a rickety four-foot tower of hardcovers and paperbacks had been piled straight up on their sides. There was one small window toward the top of the end wall, facing out toward the volleyball area. Light showed from underneath the bathroom door. Ev found the switch on the wall and flicked it on.

A sound came from behind the door, the straining grunt of a constipated man slaving over a long awaited bowel movement.

"I'm on ze toilet!"

"Visitor's waitin' you," Ev piped up.

"Tell him I will meet him in the lounge."

Ev nodded down at me, making with the shorthand, then he backed out of the room and disappeared. I hesitated a moment, then went out after him but couldn't face the prospect of sitting through a Kamikaze movie with a roomful of zombies, not even five minutes of it. I much preferred the earthy music of my idol grunting or passing gas. Somehow, I found the thought of it endearing; after all, at times, it's childishly difficult for us to imagine the great or beautiful doing normal things. For myself, the fact that I had caught Wilde with his pants down, so to speak, made him all the more spectacular. There was no need for artifice or promotion. Here was a man whose life was his art, whose art was his life.

7

I was possessed with the glory of the moment, that is until the bathroom door opened and he stepped out with a bottle of Glenlivet dangling from his right hand. The half-full bottle was backlit by the bathroom light and shined golden. The second he saw me, he frowned. He didn't look drunk. His eyes were bright and canny and he didn't sway. His thin mouth became an expressionless straight line. Then his eyes crinkled slightly. They censored me, staring; finally, they rolled up and down somewhat drolly as he raised the Glenlivet by the neck and took a healthy chug. I could tell he thought I'd been sent to spy on him. He lowered the bottle and banged it down on top of the card table.

"Mr. Wilde, I can't tell you what a—"

"Spies are fools and fools are clowns. Clowns belong in the circus."

Yep, I was right. "I was just waiting to see you, sir," I said shakily, hamming up the solicitude. It wasn't hard. I wanted to talk to the man, get to know him, and right now my foot was barely in the door and he was ready to throw me out.

Wilde threw back his small robust shoulders and ran a hand through his handsome mop of wavy white hair. He pulled up the sleeves of his V-neck cashmere sweater and sat down at the table, pretending to study the few cards that were left there. The hair on his chest and hands matched his head. His black loafers had tassels, the only adornment.

"I'm drunk. It's bad that I am drunk. Tell me, then you may go tell them, and they can cancel the picture. Ha!" he laughed. Wilde was Austro-Hungarian. He'd grown up in Vienna and spent his early years with UFA in Berlin. There wasn't much of a trace of an accent, except for his way of speaking from the back of his throat, somewhat like Maurice Chevalier. Women probably went for it.

"Please, Mister Wilde, I'm one of your biggest fans," I urged him. "I really am. I've seen *The Boulevard* over a hundred times. What you do with light—"

The master nodded. "Like the impressionists, only without color. Color is ugly, gaudy. It distracts from form—you see?"

"Of course."

He grabbed hold of the bottle and suspicion creased his brow. "It's easy to say you liked *The Boulevard*. Butter me up. How many times have you seen N, *The Great Impersonator*, films like this, hmm? They don't mention these—" Here, he made a treading motion with his free hand as his mind searched for words. "—in *The Filmgoer's Companion*."

Wilde pursed his lips, giving *The Filmgoer's Compan-*

ion a quick raspberry. So then I had to have it out with him. I gave him the full casts and credits for all of his major films and many of the obscure ones. I recounted the legendary difficulties he'd had with Crawford, Fontaine, and Harlow. I discussed his strengths and weaknesses from the pencilheaded critics' point of view, meanwhile amending and elaborating from my own perspective. I paraded my thesis that he was indeed the true father of *film noir* and backed it up with discursive points to explain why. Wilde listened and drank. His face remained intelligent but impassive.

After twenty minutes of this one-sided monologue, he told me to get up and close the door. Then he told me to pick up a fresh pack of cards by the books on the nightstand. I brought them back to the table and Wilde started shuffling.

After a minute, Ev came back and asked if I'd been jivin' about the patient leaving through the front door. I assured him that I hadn't. He took Wilde's bottle, grabbed a quick shot, then handed it back. "That's bad," he said. Then he left.

Wilde continued shuffling and proceeded to give me his analysis of the escapee's problems. I was told his name was Bruce Spindel, age thirty-three, an excellent bridge player with Master's points, and a perfectly normal homosexual, married to the same man for ten years but subject to depressive episodes when exposed to his mother. Mom had threatened to kill herself if sonny boy moved far away.

"A problem with affect," Wilde rambled on. "*Affect.* She shows nothing, appears to hate the child, yet she says she loves him and would not know what to do without him—never to his face, of course—on the telephone, at half past three in ze morning. She begs him to come over, then when he arrives she must prove how she doesn't need him to survive. This is why the young man is here. He will not be free until he kills his parent, yet if he does so, he kills himself. I have suggested that he dye his hair, have plastic surgery on ze face, and move to Caracas."

At this, Wilde threw his head back and laughed like a trained seal does when it wants fish. I started suspecting his sanity. The two of us were supposed to work together. I thought of that and threw my head back and joined him.

Wilde's laugh switch flipped the other way suddenly. His jaw dropped with brooding sullenness. For the first time, his eyes showed confusion. They shifted restlessly about, in rhythm with the spasmodic quiet noises just outside the room.

"There's no escaping," the great man said softly, lowering his head. "Impossible. . . . we cannot appease them. . . . The ghosts, they stick us, then pick, they pick at our scabs. There is no healing!"

"Yeah, yeah, sure." What could I say?

Abruptly, Wilde looked up, handed me the cards, and told me to deal out gin rummy. He asked if I knew how to keep score for three across, then grinned demoniacally as I nodded, took the scratch pad, and made my columns and boxes. I was fooling myself. I knew it. This man was in no shape to work with anybody, yet I kept thinking he was about to settle down. As I dealt, he mumbled to himself and shook his head. His forehead was beaded with perspiration and the virile white mane was losing its wave and bounce and taking on an oily, matted look. The brightness in his eyes was drying into a dull, lusterless glaze. Rarely have I ever resisted a proffered fifth of anything, but the taste for drink had been drained out of me as I sat there before this wreck of ruined genius.

"Ghosts. . . . Dead, dead. . . . Reeking, why?!"

He was far too old to take to the stage, especially as Hamlet. "Mister Wilde?" I said gently.

He picked up his hand and arranged the cards. "Have some schnapps," he ordered me.

The stuff could have been arsenic for all the appeal it possessed for me. "No. Upset stomach," I said into my cards.

He didn't want the knock card. I passed on it myself. He drew first, applauding his choice with the sort of lip-licking leer that a fetishist would use when perusing his monthly *Frederick's of Hollywood* lingerie catalog. He discarded with a sigh, snapping the corner of the card as he laid it down.

"We will play much gin," Alfie said quietly from behind his hand. "The excitement of the right card is like finding the right idea, the right word, what makes the story click." Alfie snapped his fingers. "Discard." He kept snapping his fingers. Liked the sound.

I played. Alfie talked. When I agreed with him or tried to add something, he smiled wolfishly. "On the contrary," he'd say for no reason.

He was obsessing over his father, who would have had to be at least eighty-five. Beautiful women had loved Alfie, but had his father? No. Parents were bigger children than children. Alfie thanked God that he'd never been a parent. Yes, he had fathered children, but he had never parented them. There was a difference. His children ran free, uncaged. He had no idea where most of them were.

There was one moment of lucidity. I'll never forget it. "The worst thing about establishing a reputation," Alfie said slowly, measuring out the exact words, "is having to live up to it. This is both unnatural and impossible. An artist's work is always changing—both in form and quality—he gets better, he gets worse; most of all he does things differently. A few are geniuses, they reek of it, and everything they do reflects their brilliance. For the rest of us, we have our moments when many factors catalyze—I think that is the word—and the artistic product appears, poof! We can't sustain that. It should not be expected. It is not possible!"

There was a pause. Neither of us said anything.

"You never know when it will stop or recommence," he continued quietly. "That is why we continue . . . but it is too hard, living up to this reputation . . . despicable. Luckily, for me, they confuse my good and bad. They accept everything. It is a joke, a sick joke."

I had four twos, three queens, and a pair of sevens. The knock card was a three. I needed gin. We were almost through the deck. Alfie started getting nervous again. His eyes jumped back and forth, he stared at blank spots on the wall as he chugged at the bottle. It was nearly empty now and rattled against his teeth as his shaky hand held it to his mouth. He went back to mumbling about ghosts and how they picked your scabs. It didn't make a bit of sense to me and I was relieved when Alfie finally got his card. The bottle was empty by then. When he slapped his hand down atop the little vinyl-covered table, the bottle bounced and slid off onto the floor.

Alfie stood up and pounded the cards with an open right hand. "Gin, gin!" he exulted.

I smiled and started gathering up the cards to deal a second hand. But he was gone. He raised his arms in victory and pranced about the table in a circle, skipping every other step.

"Gin! Gin!!" he kept screaming.

I saw his cards for a moment before he bumped into the table and knocked them to the floor. Three tens and a four-through-nine run in diamonds. I had the seven of diamonds. His seven was a heart. Oh, well.

Alfie ripped off his cashmere sweater and mopped his sweating face. Then he looked at me with raised eyebrows like he'd forgotten I was there. He smiled at me like one of his long lost sons, put his arms around my middle and hugged me hard as he buried his face in my shoulder. I felt drunk as I inhaled his breath. Luckily, he broke the clinch and stood back from me, nodding sagely.

"We will make a great picture," he pronounced. Then, instantly, he wheeled about and screamed toward the window. "No!!!"

I have never seen wilder eyes or heard a voice charged with so much terror. Alfie covered his face and fell back toward the bed. His fists clenched, his short arms flailed about, punching the empty air. It was coming at him through the dark space of that window. Before I could reach the door, Ev and another male orderly rushed in from the hall. A sloe-eyed young blonde followed them in. She had a fat hypo in her hand which detracted from her short skirt.

I got the hell out of there. My idol, I decided, was truly one of the craziest bastards I'd ever met. He was way beyond the sort of collaboration that involved working on a script. This man couldn't have cared less about making a movie. He was trying to get out of one, the one inside his head.

8

"**G**ood, baby, good. You got it. . . . Yeah, push . . . faster . . . around . . . good . . . slow, again, now."

It was 10:15 PM. Sam was standing upside down with her head on a pillow. Her legs were wrapped about my waist and her back was braced up against two corner walls of the bridal suite in the Santa Barbara Biltmore. It was a difficult position, but the rush upon orgasm was supposed to run neck to neck with freebase cocaine or amyl nitrite. I didn't care. Sam liked it in hot tubs and Jacuzzis, over refrigerated waterbeds, on Quaaludes with herbal tea—I don't know, it was all just fine as far as I was concerned. After a while, she either relaxed and shut up or I was so into it I didn't care. I stood there, leaning over her, pumping and squeezing her moon-faced ass. Her lively breasts were bobbling backwards toward her shoulders, her face looked odd from upside down, but then she stopped orchestrating all the movements and we got going. We were banging the hell out of each other when the phone rang.

"I better get that," she said throatily.

"Fuck it." I kept the heat on.

Someone gave the wall a few discreet taps from the other side. As the phone was still squalling, that's all it took to break the spell. I stopped squeezing and let her go. My hands left red marks over her pale buttocks. She looked dizzy as she made her way to the phone. I walked over to the champagne bucket and poured a few last drops into my glass.

"Hello," her voice chimed with early morning brightness. "I was in the middle of something. . . . What's wrong, Bernie?"

Bernie Marks, our dear president. Sam's voice had lost its freewheeling timbre. It sounded serious. She got her Shermans and lit up.

"But I don't see how that's possible," she was saying. "I'm with Ben. He was just there a few hours ago." Sam took the phone from her ear and held it out toward me. "Alfie Wilde committed suicide," she said blankly. "He left the hospital. They found him in some gin mill. Bernie wants to talk to you."

I couldn't say I was surprised. I came over and Sam handed me the phone. "Yes, Mister Marks."

"You saw Alfie?" asked a voice that was all business, not a hint of shakiness or sunken feelings in its husky baritone.

"Yeah, I did. About six o'clock."

"Did he seem crazy?"

"As a loon, sir."

"That's not very respectful language for a man of his reputation."

"He was a great man, but you asked me a question, didn't you?"

"Give me Sam," he said gruffly.

Sam got back on the line. I sat on the bed and rubbed her back. From listening to her side of the conversation, it seemed like Bernie was talking about Alfie's picture and worrying about what they were going to do. Sam said the script was "adequate." There were problems with it, but, as already discussed, they could be ironed out. My name was brought up as the one who was supposed to do the ironing. Then Marks started asking questions about me because Sam's replies turned short and clipped. She shrugged me away, got up and started pacing the floor at the foot of the bed. Her compact little thigh muscles were tense and lovely.

"Yes . . . yes . . . I assure you he can. . . . That's right. . . . Well, I think so." Then: "No, no, no," rapid fire and quite adamantly, a pause, then: "Bernie, I assure you, that has nothing to do with it," ending coyly with, "Well, maybe just a little."

I got up to take a shower. Alfie Wilde had committed suicide. How, I wondered—the wrists, a gun, an OD. What did it matter? I tried to shake the morbid thoughts out of my head. It was unreal. Not that Alfie was dead, but the matter-of-fact way his death was being accepted. Bernie Marks was one tough cookie, that was for sure. And what about Sam, what about me? This was business, that was all. Alfie's offing himself was a business proposition, and it had to be dealt with in a businesslike manner. Sentiment was not even a consideration here. Sentiment would be left to . . . ? Yes, sentiment was definitely one big question mark. I turned the dial on the shower head to *Massage* and let the hard warm water pound my neck and back. I thought of Question Mark and Mysterions. They'd had a hit song, "Ninety-six Tears." "I'm gonna cry ninety-six tears, I'm gonna cry ninety-six tears . . . I'm gonna cry, cry, cry now." The backup music sounded like a drunken convention of organ grinders and hurdy-gurdy men. Who the hell would cry for Alfie Wilde? Shit, no wonder he was dead.

By the time I had turned off the shower, Sam had entered the bathroom. She was grabbing up all of her toiletries and dumping them into her cosmetic case, moving like a whirling dervish.

"I gotta be at Bernie's in two hours," she said.

"Does that mean we're leaving?"

"You can stay if you like." She stopped with a bottle of perfume in her hand. For a moment, I thought she was going to throw it at me; then she dropped it in the case, came over and wrapped her arms around my waist. "Babe, we got an emergency on our hands," she said.

I pulled her to me and tried to start up where we'd left off. Without another word, she yanked herself away and, giving me a look that could have split atoms, went back to the packing with redoubled fury. I got dressed and called down to room service for a bottle of Glenlivet. I was feeling sentimental, guilty too. I had been one of the last people to see Alfie Wilde alive. Could I have done anything, said the wrong thing, been insensitive to a cry for help, some subtle nuance in what he'd been saying to me? Had I ticked him off? I didn't think so, still, I wasn't sure and I was going to toast him with the fire-water that had killed him. That didn't seem sympathetic, but I wanted Alfie to know I could begin to understand him. Sure, he'd been a lunatic for the few seconds I'd known him. Some people were crazier than Alfie, some less crazy. Keeping in mind the vague *Hamlet* theme he'd laid down, maybe there had been some method to his madness. Hard to say. I'd probably never quite get a grip on that, but as Alfie had said, being Alfie Wilde was a damn hard thing to live up to.

When Room Service knocked, I opened the door to

an aged, little beak-nosed bellhop. The Glenlivet was on an ornate silver tray with two glasses and an ice bucket. The little guy was polishing the dusty bottle with one of his goldbanded green cuffs. I took the tray from him, set it down on the carpet inside the door, picked up the bottle and both glasses, handed him one and poured us each a healthy drink. He stepped inside when I put the glass in his hand. Sam was standing with her back to us, bent naked over her suitcase. A fresh lit pink Sherman hung sideways from her languid mouth.

"I, I'm sorry," the little fella stuttered, starting to back out.

I grabbed his sleeve. "Hey, it's OK," I told him. "You know us, from the sexy sixties, through the swinging seventies, to the enlightened eighties?"

Sam frowned over her shoulder, then returned to her packing.

"Take it easy," I assured him.

He smiled unhappily and froze to the carpet as I closed the door. "Sure is different today," he said.

I clicked glasses with him. "You can say that again," I said meaninglessly.

The little guy's hand shook as he raised his glass and swallowed the contents in one swift jolt. "Well, thank you very much, sir, ma'am," he said, handing me his glass and grabbing for the door knob. "I hope you have a very happy honeymoon . . . or whatever."

I raised my glass to the little man as he backed into the hall, blinking his gray eyes and wiping the sweat off his forehead.

"That was mean," Sam told me as I shut the door.

"To you or to him?"

"You're going to get drunk, aren't you?"

Yeah, I was. That's what it was all about. I felt mean. Everybody deserved a good jolt. Especially those who didn't expect it. They needed it. Sam called me a big baby and walked around the room, pulling out all the drawers and checking for forgotten items as she got dressed. The Glenlivet was like dead man's bile. I couldn't drink more than one shot of it. It was the smell of Wilde's sweat. It depressed me. I left the bottle on the bureau. Sam seemed surprised. Served her right.

We checked out. Sam paid the bill. The pear-bellied desk man had a zipped up tiny mouth in an otherwise hugely round face. His eyes studied one of my shoulders as Sam signed the charge ticket. Tired of entertaining, I gave myself the hook and walked out quickly before I could think of something funny to do to him.

9

If I'd had any chance of fazing Sam, it was dashed to bits by the time she settled in behind the wheel of her precious Berlinetta Boxer. Sam was always happy in her shiny little $100,000 Ferrari. But it was more than that. She would have done anything to get on with the show. Good cheer and cooperation make for well-oiled efficiency and she was determined to get along with me, at least until we got home. I could have let this drive me bug-eyed with exasperation; instead, I met nonchalance with nonchalance and fell asleep in my deep bucket seat listening to the monotonous high purr of the expensive engine.

When I woke up, I was proud of myself, thinking I'd one-upped her. No such luck. Samantha Kovac's conviction was genuine. It wasn't hastily manufactured to meet the demands of the moment. In all things she was casual. She kept a level head which made her infinitely desirable for both business and sex. She had more, she could do more. You couldn't help but feel it. Even so, regardless of her position and stockholdings, she was still somebody's yes man. She kowtowed and jumped to it when Bernie snapped his callous egomaniacal fingers. There was a certain chilliness about this that sent shivers through me. I had been living in Sam's world for some time now, but this was the first bird's-eye view I felt I'd had of it. To Sam and Bernie Marks, Alfie Wilde was a business proposition, a mark on a profit-loss statement, an entry in the monthly agenda at the board meeting. That BS she'd given me about wanting to preserve Wilde's great reputation, that's exactly what it was: BS, quoth the raven, BS.

I told her that I thought she was a callous, brown-nosing opportunist and general all-around exploiter, and, instead of downshifting into fourth and swerving over to the roadside by Oxnard, she looked at me with pity in her dark eyes, patted my head, and worked her long fingers into the tension knots in my neck and shoulders. She understood, so she said. I was a writer, of course I'd take Wilde's death to heart. It meant more to me—but that didn't mean it wasn't affecting her. She couldn't relate to death, that was her problem, she said, so she buried herself in her work.

Maybe so. Who was I to say? Sam's problem keyed right in to what Alfie had been saying about lack of affect. It seemed to be all around us. Never more to see and experience, never less to take it in with. How could this be explained? Maybe what we were crying out for was a fresh new administration, somebody mean and nasty to take it to those dirty oilbearers. Maybe so.

BS, quoth the raven, BS. I was thinking like a drunkard and I wasn't even drunk. I started warming up to Sam's neck rub. I don't think there's another human being on the face of this earth who can drive an Italian car at 100 miles per hour and give you a muscle-relaxing rub worthy of an Oriental massage parlor, both at the same time. With Sam, it was possible. She'd had a lifetime of training. I'd never known her to do less than two things at the same time.

We got to Malibu in what seemed like five minutes and pulled into Sam's beach house. I wanted a quickie so bad I could taste it, but by the time I followed her inside, her houseboy, William, was already handing her the phone. I shoved my hands in my pockets and paced around staring at the walls as Sam disappeared down the straight hall, jabbering orders out of my hearing.

"How are you?" the spry young fellow asked me.

A self-professed gigolo to his friends, he was a male model who liked to say he was an art student at UCLA. Sam had once owned him. I think that was his biggest claim to fame. Now, he tidied up and did the cooking in return for room and board. I think he modeled himself after the Richard Gere character in the recent Hollywood movie about a high class gigolo. He drove a shiny Mercedes 450 SL, wore the fancy, slightly formal clothes, and had that vampish, jaded, bored look about him which, as properly applied, goes hand in hand with a well honed physique, an even tan, and a wellcapped ready smile—the consummate Don Juan who, shattered soul that he is, alas, can do nothing but administer pleasure without receipt of same.

"Lack of affect," so it seemed to me at the moment.

"Excuse me?"

"I think you're suffering from a lack of affect," I told him.

He raised his head rather dreamily and looked at me with sad, red-rimmed eyes. "I know. I'm in therapy," he said blandly. "Can I get you anything?"

"Yes, I'd like two Quaaludes, six lines, and some mild Colombian," I said.

"Coming right up." He turned toward the kitchen.

"Hold it. On second thought, you got any J.D.?"

"J.D.?"

"Jack Daniels."

"Sure."

"Well, just some of that."

I sat down by the fire in the livingroom and admired the Lichtensteins and Warhols for the second they deserved. Then I sacked out over the long couch and waited for my medicine. William came on soundless feet and set the glass before me on a square black coaster. I picked it up and took a long sip.

"Ah," I said.

He took that as an invitation to conversation. "Good for the affect," he said.

I looked up and smiled at him. "I'm a very sensitive guy, William. I got so much affect I don't know what to do with it." I held up the glass. "This is making mincemeat out of my affect."

"Exactly what you want."

"Exactly, William, exactly."

I finished the drink and asked William for more. He came out of the kitchen wearing a long white apron and carrying a bottle of Old Bushmills. I didn't want Bushmills, I wanted more J.D., but there wasn't any left; so I laid back down and listened to William run the rinse water and clatter the pots and pans. Sam had disappeared behind her bedroom door. I could hear the muted rise and fall of her business voice. I lay there pretending I wasn't waiting around, thinking I was enjoying a good rest; eventually, I sat up. Who was I fooling, lying there with a hard on and an empty whiskey glass?

I got up and went out to my car. The fucker wouldn't

start. I opened up the hood and smoke came out of it. I went back into the house, marched down the hall, and barged into Sam's bedroom. Phone in hand, she had changed into a conservative dark green twill woven suit and was sitting on the edge of the silver satin quilt covering the bed. She was smoking a plain Sherman and staring out at the night. The choppy tide wrapped itself around the pilings just below, making a whooshing din that sounded like a roomful of consumptives trying to blow out candles. Sam was making headway, plowing through the sloth of her sleepy subordinate with a honied sure voice that cut calmly but ferociously, like a laser.

"Of course he's an ass," she was crooning, "but he wants us there a half an hour ago. . . . He's afraid of the bank . . . I know, but can't you see—"

"My car broke down," I broke in loudly.

Sam looked at me over her shoulder and crossed her legs. When I stepped over to her, I saw that neither of her feet touched the plush floor. She said something meaningless into the phone and told whoever she was talking with to hold on.

She looked at me pityingly and rubbed her hand up and down my crotch. "Poor baby. Your nostrils are flaring. Take the Boxer, but you have to drop it off for servicing—eight o'clock."

I backed away and frowned. "I don't need a booby prize. I just want to go home. I'm tired. Let me take the Caddie."

She shook her head. "No gas." She dug into her purse and tossed me her keys. "Or have William drive you." She took her hand off the phone as she blew me a kiss and whispered, "Don't be mad. I'll call you tomorrow."

I stormed out of the room and got out of that house. I wasn't going to let William drive me. The last thing I

needed was to be chauffeured home by a snobbish po-
seur gigolo who spent all of his free time cultivating looking lonely because he knew there was money in it. Ugh!
There I was, horny and depressed with a broken down
car; Alfie Wilde, a great man I had just met, was now a
suicide statistic and a media scoop for the morning news
and my girl friend had willfully succumbed to coitus interruptus in order to kowtow to her boss, who was in a
panic to discuss the event's monetary repercussions.

Well, fuck them all! I crawled into the Ferrari. The
engine revved into a high whine that seemed to mimic
the strident one-sided argument in my mind's stage center. It was like giving a contender a million bucks and
throwing him in the ring with strict instructions to beat
himself up. Sure, you can flagellate yourself, and it does
get you somewhere—because *you know* you're right—
but then, again, it doesn't. The world stinks and you're
a goddamn prince—but what's the diff? You're still livin'
in it.

I screamed my way out onto the Pacific Coast Highway in first gear. The light fog bounced the high beams
back in my face and muffled every sound. By the time I
hit second, I was going eighty-five. Somewhat like fucking, but not quite. Five minutes later I was up the Wilshire ramp and idling out in front of a closed liquor store
on Ocean Avenue. I hopped out of the car and knocked
on the glass door as a slouchy, gray-faced guy with a
broad mashed-in nose frowned at me and turned the
sign around to *Closed*. Then he saw the Ferrari. His
vague eyes brightened behind dirty hornrims. He
smacked his dry lips, rubbed a sleeve across his mouth,
and nodded approvingly toward the car as he started
turning away.

"Give ya a ride!" I yelled through to him.

He turned back around and regarded me with suspicion. I nodded up and down. When all was said and done, he settled for a short drive and the change to a twenty and I ended up with an open fifth of J.D. in my hand. The guy was an aged hotrodder. He spent the whole ride lecturing me on the inferiority of foreign cars and criticizing my shifting. I couldn't get it going fast enough for him, and he walked away in a huff when I let him off.

I continued north on Ocean, skirting the narrow length of parkway that runs along the high bluff above the Pacific Coast Highway. It was 1:00 AM and the street was deserted. The wind was chilling down the fake summer air and sending a briny smelling breeze through the open windows of the car. Overhead, the big palm trees rustled their fronds, an amazon army swishing their grass skirts and coming after me in a hurry. I turned onto San Vicente Boulevard and emerged from the fog cover by the time I got up to Sunset. I drove along through Brentwood and Bel-Air, swigging at the bottle and trying to relax. But the sea air, fog, and changing weather had me all worked up, that and my unconscionable coitus interruptus. It made me think of a Polack joke Sam had told me: "Did you hear about the Polack actress? She fucked the writer." You see, you'd have to be dumber than a used Brillo pad to think you could get anywhere *that* way.

I think it was driving Sam's car that made me so maudlin. I wanted to get away from her, but I couldn't. The faster I swerved along, the whinier the engine shriek. She was taunting me. She was on my back. Was this the way I wanted to live? Was this love? Why, I hardly even knew her and yet I'd been delighting in trying to convince her to marry me. She knew better.

"Getting to know you . . . getting to know you . . ."

I was halfway through the hooch, winding through

"The Strip" by Tower Records. Wisps of white smoke were funneling out over the top of gaudy yellow and red neon flames on a new music billboard. The name of the album was "Hot 'N' Smokin'. " Further on, movie extravaganzas were touted, Vegas hotels bragged about their weekend specials. Some of them did it with sequins that glittered in the spotlights, others had figures with moving arms and legs. They were predictably cluttered and overstated, never simple or refined; but you always looked forward to seeing what they'd do next, and they never failed to disappoint or insult you.

There was something wistful and nostalgic about it all. I felt like sitting at a piano bar and telling somebody to jiggle the ivories over "The Days of Wine and Roses." No, maybe Dylan's "The Times They Are A Changin'. " Could you jiggle any ivories over that? No, and that was exactly why the song had been an anthem of sorts—just because you couldn't. It could never be sung or played in piano bars or made into Muzak. You had to strum that dirge on a guitar that had a peace symbol painted on it and belt it out with a clothespin clamped over your nose. They'd done it that way in college. Peace, peace, peace—they'd all wanted peace; then they got some and it seemed like there was nothing left to do. Peace wasn't "in" anymore. Now, decadence, S/M, and making oodles of dough were what made people's hearts throb. The new punk generation did the pogo dance to work themselves up into a violent state, trying to stimulate their lost affects 'cause they'd lost 'em. Life had become garish and exaggerated. "Sex and drugs and rock 'n' roll," that was some song and we all needed lots, more and more of it, anything loud and strong, whatever it took to stir up that slothful, put-up-in-mothballs affect.

"Where have all the affects gone, long time ago? Where have all the affects gone—long time passing?"

Peaceniks, punks—I didn't need any of it. People were always oppressive, no matter what they did. Dylan was oppressive. Now, I'd heard hc wanted to save us all with Jesus. You couldn't get away from it. Somebody always wanted to tell you what to do. Fuck 'em! I went back to "The Days of Wine and Roses," singing it and thinking it was the best song I'd ever heard, when I passed her out in front of Le Dome, across the street from Cyrano's. She was walking up the street toward Ben Frank's all-night coffee shop. I couldn't have missed her. Dressed in red, purple, and glittering gold, this one made the Whore of Babylon look like a spinster school teacher.

I pulled right over, flung open the door on the passenger side, and asked her how she was doing this evening. She had toothpick legs on six-inch stiletto heels that made her look like she was tottering on stilts. Her tits and hair were of the Dolly Parton variety. I handed her the bottle and told her to have a drink. She said something cute in a high-pitched baby doll voice and stroked my hand as she leaned forward and took the bottle. One of her big tits bulged out of the dress. I fell back and guffawed; she giggled politely. She had enough wrinkle lines to string up a kite and was the oldest whore I'd seen in these parts for an awfully long time. I thought she was cute. When she stepped down into Sam's car, I squeezed her a bit and kissed her sloppily over her mouth and ears.

Then I revved up and headed for home. She asked me if I wanted to have a party and I dared her to take her clothes off in the car. In a second, we were up the canyon. She squinted at my dump like it was so small she couldn't see it. Confusing. Folks with $100,000 cars just don't tend to live in little beat-up canyon shanties; so I started in on this song and dance about how my mansion was being remodeled. This dumb writer friend of mine was out of town and I was staying in his little dump for a week or so because I absolutely loathed hotels. My God, I was in form, I was rolling, I was doubling down. Gail, that was her name. I wanted her cheap ass so badly I would have married her and suffered alimony just to own her for the next half hour.

I got out of the car with the bottle and went around to help her out. She took the red scarf off her shoulders, wrapped it around the back of my neck, and pulled me toward her. We smooched. I squeezed her some more and ran my hands through her pearly platinum hair. It was fine, sticky, wooly—like cotton candy. I told her I wanted to eat it and she looked pleased, but her eyes were cautious and rather civilized; her mouth, too, looked thoughtful, slightly perplexed. She looked like somebody trying to find their way out of a house of mirrors. This only made me sorry for her, so I kept squeezing her and blubbered in her ear about how happy I was going to make her. Then I picked her up in my arms and staggered up the short stairs to the house. Her costume bracelets and necklaces jingled all the way as she started in on questions, what I did, where I really lived. I parried them all with the utmost of ease, meanwhile feeling her ass from below. It wasn't tiny and she wasn't light either. I tried not to wheeze for breath as I set her down before the door.

10 ....

I killed the bottle and dropped it in the bushes. She put her arms around my waist, so I pushed her up against the door, smooched her, and we started dry-humping. She bleated out the phoniest moan of ecstasy I'd ever heard; I stopped and unlocked the kitchen front door, hoping there was more J.D. in store. Stanley let out a little howl from inside and I could have sworn he was trying to make fun of her. Then I remembered that the kid would be sound asleep by now and made the hush sign as I started walking on my tiptoes. Gail seemed to find this amusing. A flourish of trilling little giggles issued from her lips. She sounded like a diva warming up. I felt like applauding. Stanley was swishing his tail and crawling around in between our feet. I told him to go in his basket beneath the kitchen table. I peeked through the beaded curtains into Petey's bedroom in the livingroom, saw a lump in the bed. then forgot about the booze and took my woman into my cave on the other side of the house.

"I'm gonna give it to ya," I was telling her. "Ooo, ooo," she was cooing.

We were all over each other. I flicked on the desk lamp and tilted it toward the floor. I started slipping her plush dress up over her head.

"What's that?" she squealed, pointing toward the bed.

I whipped around and looked.

"Hi, Ben."

I turned on the overhead light. Petey was lying in the center of my bed. He rubbed his eyes and sat up, trying to plant the usual tough guy grin in his face. It came out sheepish and he had something to be sheepish about: there was a twelve-year-old girl sleeping on either side of him. One of them stirred and turned over, the other was sleeping on her side, facing me with her thumbnail in her mouth. She had long, lanky hair, the other a short pageboy. They were both brunettes, skinny little tomboys; their pale shoulders glowed under the ceiling lights. Petey still had freckles on his. Whatever drunkenness I'd felt vanished into thin air. It was like a cop had pulled me over and ordered me out to walk the line—bam, you're tense and sober.

"Why, you little monkey," I began portentously.

That got a rise out of the side of his mouth. He reached for his Kools, tapped one out, and stuck it in his face sideways. He was reaching for a match when I stepped up to the bed and grabbed it out of his mouth.

"Hey!" he remonstrated.

I crumbled the cigarette and dropped it on the floor. "What the hell do you think you're doing?!" I yelled at him.

The sleeping girls sat up with a jolt. The long-haired one was completely flat chested; the pageboy had little budding breasts. They pulled the sheet up to cover themselves.

"Peter!"

"Pete, what's goin' on?" they twittered.

"What does it look like?" the kid was saying as he went to his pack for another Kool.

"You get out of that bed," I ordered him.

"No."

"Get up." I turned my attention to the girls. "Get up and put your clothes on."

The little girls clung to the sheet, sat there with their knees up, petrified. I bore in on Petey. My stare was hot enough to fry an egg. "Now you get up out of there, mister. Or am I gonna have to drag you?"

"We were just sleeping!" the pageboy said with a simpering pout.

"Yeah," the long-haired one chipped in.

I turned and glared at her. She was biting her bottom lip.

"We weren't doin' nothin'," Petey said with Brando-esque taciturnity.

"How old are you?!" I bellowed at him.

He scowled back at me, saying nothing as he curled the side of his mouth with disdain.

"Thirteen," I answered for him. "And what about you or you," I demanded, pointing at his partners in sin. "Eleven, twelve?"

"I'm thirteen," the flat-chested one almost cried, pulling the sheet up over most of her face.

"What are your names?"

They looked at each other. Neither spoke.

"You ain't gotta say nothin'," Petey assured them with a sagelike nod.

"Well, you can corrupt anybody else you want," I informed them, "but you stay away from my son."

"I ain't your son," he said.

"You shut your fuckin' mouth."

I leaned over the long-haired girl, took him by the arm, and yanked him off the bed. The girls grabbed the sheet back to their chins and held on for dear life. His pants were on the floor in the center of the room. I walked him over to them, leaned over and picked them up. My "party" was standing on the end of one of the pant legs.

"Excuse me," I told her, having forgotten she was there.

She stepped aside as I grabbed up the jeans and shoved them at the kid. "Get your ass in these," I ordered him. Then, turning back toward the bed: "And you get out of there, get dressed. I'm taking you home to meet your parents."

Then I took my gaudy woman by the hand and stormed out of the room, slamming the door.

Due to this new set of circumstances, the lovey-dovey mood was broken and neither of us had a thing to say to each other. I was rummaging around in the cupboards, looking for something else to drink, when the kid opened the bedroom door and came through the bathroom to the far edge of the kitchen. He had his jeans on and was wearing the fancy pair of snakeskin boots I'd given him as another one of his Christmas presents. He stood there nervously combing his hair for a moment, then he took a puff on the cigarette he'd been holding behind his back. After that, he squared his narrow shoulders, took a deep breath, and looked at me with bitter hatred steaming from his moist eyes. He jerked his head toward my Queen of Sheba.

"What's her name?"

"That's no way to refer to a lady," I told him.

Stanley didn't like the sound of this. He crawled out of his basket and snuck off to the bedroom, his long nails tapping the floor. Petey stood his ground and gestured toward me with his cigarette hand.

"What makes you so fuckin' perfect, huh, Ben?"

"I'm thirty-four, you're thirteen," I said roughly.

"You're full of shit," he said, backing away to give himself a head start in case I came after him.

I gave him the head start, then I lumbered back to the bedroom. The girls were gone. They'd crawled out the window. In no uncertain terms, I proceeded to tell the kid what I thought of him. I told him off like he was an adult, not a child. I was so steamed up, I don't even remember what I said, but the theme of it had to do with his ungratefulness and the fact, according to me, that I was a better father than he deserved. I only wished he were a better son. When I was finished, I went back into the kitchen. My woman was gone. I went outside and walked down the hill, looking for her, then I came back, got the car and drove down the canyon. I couldn't find her.

When I got back to the house, Petey was gone too. He had taken Stanley. Chances were he had gone off on a long walk to calm down, although the distinct possibility that he had run away again couldn't be dismissed either.

Well, I decided that was his business. For the moment, I was fed up. I sat down at the table and brooded. What a night. What a night . . .

11

But it wasn't over. I found another bottle underneath the sink, behind the wastebasket, sat back down at the table and tried to figure out how it had gotten there. Memory confirmed that I had put it there myself in a one-man hide-and-seek game I'd organized a few weeks past when I'd arrived at a crucial juncture in my rewrite and got to feeling nippy.

"Should of tied a string around it and hung it out the window," I told no one.

I had one short drink that somehow wouldn't taste right, no matter how I swallowed or swilled it around, then I just sat at the table some more pretending like I wasn't waiting again. I'd been doing a lot of that lately. Finally, I went out to the car and drove around the canyon looking for Petey. No luck.

I ended up on Santa Monica Boulevard around two o'clock. Something drove me to the ticket window of the Pussycat Theatre. I had to walk through an uninspired picket line of three or four young men and four or five decrepit couples carrying small placards hardly larger than the cardboard backs the laundry sticks in your shirts. The old men were balding and bespectacled, the women wan and blue-haired. The young men were nattily attired in three-piece rack suits. One of them had a small flash camera hanging around his neck. Their banners read: *Make Hollywood The Sin Capital; Pornography Belongs In Hollywood, Its Birthplace.*

I'd never seen people campaigning *for* porno, especially old folks before a porno theater. Considering their bandwagon, you would have thought they'd walk up to me and shake my hand. I turned and studied them for a moment, long enough to tell me that this was clearly not the case. One of the young men gestured toward me, smiled in my direction, and started forward, but he was stopped by a little, straight-backed, blue-haired dowager who looked at me like I'd instantly transmogrified into a hundred and ninety-five pound glob of greenish phlegm. She looked away, turning her placard toward a small pack of late-night cruisers slouching up toward the stoplight at Fairfax. Halfhearted, unintelligible oaths and objections were tossed from the cars. The light changed and they plodded on. The street turned empty.

"The crowd's gone," her old husband spoke loudly into her ear.

She was carrying a clipboard tucked under the arm of her overcoat; a pencil on a string dangled from it. She lowered her placard and took out the clipboard. Her lips moved as she counted the signatures on the petition, then they pursed tight as she shook her head and made a disapproving clucking sound I couldn't hear. I guessed that they hadn't gotten everything they'd been after.

I turned back to the ticket window and plunked down my seven bucks. The ticket guy squinted at the pickets out of baggy, red-rimmed eyes and shrugged his boney lopsided shoulders. He scratched his bald crown hard enough to remove a tick, then grunted through his nose.

"Greek to me," he said.

Greek to both of us. I turned my back on my rooting fans and went in. There was no one to take my ticket at the door to the lobby. The popcorn and candy counter was closed. I could clearly hear the simulated moans of ecstasy coming from inside the double doors to the inner sanctum. It sounded like a den of vampires exulting over a just-discovered lake of human blood. If the French referred to their orgasms as "little deaths," this stuff could only belong to the big leagues.

It was a little too much for me, but of course I went in anyway and sat toward the front. The ghosted atmosphere gave off a damp, clammy odor of cigarettes, booze, and sweat. There was no one else there. Up on the screen, a couple in wedding costume had just entered their hotel room. As the groom popped the cork off the champagne, three girls in see-through nighties came waltzing out of the closet. They greeted the bride like an old pal, which led me to the conclusion that this unlikely surprise was intended as her dowry. I couldn't believe it. Even porno was getting heavy these days; either that or I'd been living in the dark ages without knowing it.

The guy feigned a few vague expressions, then whipped his clothes off with a laugh, revealing his formidable equipment. In seconds, they were all down to nothing and sniffing each other out in all the usual permutations. I could hear my own breathing. It was heavy and my breath was whistling through my nose and sort of catching in my throat, both at the same time. I sounded like I was about to cry or something. I looked around. The darkness was close on me, sandwiching me from the back and sides. The screen, too bright, was boring through my head. The shit was giving me the creeps. I got up and got out of there.

Outside, it had started raining. That odd pro-porno picket line had gone home. Now, the rain trickled; in a half-hour or so, it would build up momentum and bully its way into a downpour that could last for an hour or two weeks if it felt like it. At this time of year in Southern California, there's no way of knowing.

I turned up my collar and got into the car. I was in a lonely, impulsive mood and couldn't face going home, so I stopped at a phone booth and looked up the address of the actress whose agent had sent me a singing telegram that afternoon out at Burbank. Grady Susan, 1205 Poinsettia Drive. You headed east on Santa Monica, past the old Sam Goldwyn Studio, and turned right down a shabby street of crumbling two-story apartments. Susan Grady's was in the middle of the block in a four unit building. The windows and doors were skirted with white metal awnings. Wet and glimmering in the streetlights, a walkway of small white hexagonal tiles started from the sidewalk and pointed straight up to the front porch in between double links of cut-down gnarly rose-bushes. A great many of the little hexagons were shattered or missing. They hadn't belonged there in the first place; they should have bordered a little rickety cottage on the beach. Some hopeful couple had been dreaming until they could afford the real thing.

I took my time wading through the rain. There were four doors, two on each side for downstairs, two in the center leading up. The left center had *Susan Grady* embossed in white capitals on a piece of shiny black tape stuck at eye height over the flat white door. I stood underneath the small awning. The rain hammered the metal above my head. I rang once, then, wary of stirring the neighbors, knocked a few more times knowing no one was there. All in all, a typical apartment for a hot new actress who was just starting to get her first breaks, I thought, stepping back onto the walk. A couple of months hence, she'd be living with some director in one of the better canyons or putting her twenty percent down on a westside condo.

Faintly, I heard tires squealing in the rain and looked out to the street as a dark, block-long Cadillac limo turned toward the curb before the tiled walk, coasted smoothly to a stop, then edged forward to center the street-side rear door into the middle of the walk. It was a recent model. Every bit of it shined—and so did she. I could see her reddish brown hair through the rear window.

I stepped over the northside row of rose stumps and waited in the dark, out of the shine of the streetlights. Two doors opened and closed, then two people came up the walk: a pudgy, baby-faced chauffeur dressed in a dark suit with a cap, carrying a wide black umbrella that caught the rain and streetlight and shadowed her shiny, copper hair.

The pudgy man wasn't tiny but he had short arms and half of his sleeve showed as he reached high to keep the umbrella over Susan Grady's head. They got to the door, a goodnight was traded for a thank you, and the chauffeur hurried back down the walk. I bided my time until the keys were found and the hall door was opened, then closed. I stepped back onto the tiled walk as the limo started up and pulled away. I walked up onto the small porch and knocked lightly. She must have been halfway up the stairs by then.

It was silent. I heard her coming back down, then stop. I knocked again to assure her that she wasn't hearing things. She continued coming down.

"Yes," she said tentatively.

"How about that drink?" I asked.

"What?"

"It's the guy who called you about the singing telegram. I know it's not Monday, but—"

Silence, then: "I'm sorry, but I just got home this minute."

Her voice was deep and husky. She couldn't help but spur me on. "I saw the limo . . . as I was driving by."

"I'm very tired."

I couldn't think of another cute line and didn't want to. I just stood there, wondering what would happen next. I had stuck my neck out. I was way out of line. That was obvious. We both knew it. Now, it was just a matter of what she intended to do about it.

"OK?" Her beautifully throaty voice came through the door, sounding exasperated.

I winced and shook my head, thinking about what an ass I was making of myself, and that's the first she saw of me, I suppose, when she suddenly pulled the door open and looked out.

I stopped and looked at her. She was beautiful, with a thin mouth that rippled nervously and magnified her tension as she smiled. She wore a mauve colored, oversized wool tam cocked over one eye. It came close to giving her a cynically confident air, that is until the hungry strained look around the mouth got further into its siren chant. Her single-strap evening gown had closely gathered horizontal pleats like an antique lampshade or theater curtain running from the floor over the top of her shoulder. A full-length lynx fur was slung over her arm. She didn't have a purse because she didn't need one. She was far beyond the type who'd require lipstick or money on her person.

She mesmerized me. I leaned forward from the waist.

She was drawing me toward her like a dumb hunk of steel. Sam had been the same way at first. So had many others. But why did this one make me feel ashamed of it? I was all out of synch tonight. I couldn't understand myself. A chill ran down my spine. I hunched my shoulders and shook my head again to get rid of it.

I must have shaken my wet hair in her face because her smallish nose twitched and she wiped it with the fur. She yanked off the tam and shook out her hair.

Her smiled broadened and pushed me back. "Lost in the rain, huh?"

"Right," I grinned.

She turned her back to me and started up the stairs. "Come on up," she said, "Hit the light."

I flicked the switch at the bottom of the stairs, the light went out, and another one came on up at the top. She had wide hips for such a slender girl and a beautiful walk that went with all the rest of her. It was hippy and she swung it side to side sexily, yet without ostentation, in such quick little arcs that, like a spinning top, the action almost sat still. My chest hurt. My forehead was cold with sweat. I felt like a junkie on the needle. I needed her. I couldn't think. I followed.

The apartment had dark wood floors that creaked. It smelled of gardenias. Dance and theater posters under glass and chrome decorated the walls. We walked into a small blue and white tiled kitchen. The floor was a neat version of the hexagonal walk outside the building. She had Glenlivet and nothing else. I opened my mouth to tell her about Alfie Wilde, but nixed that before I let myself get started. Glenlivet was my drink tonight. Yes, I wanted Glenlivet. This all probably meant something, but I wasn't crazy enough to waste my time thinking about it. My mind was all thin, pale arms and ankles, a quivering mouth, gyro hips, and an insanely sweet distillation of gardenias that seemed to float on her breath. Dizzying.

As we talked, she seemed to be studying me from various angles as if I were changing chameleonlike by the second. I could tell she was feeling me out. I must have passed the test because, though she wasn't drinking much, she started laughing rather breathlessly and sharing some confidences. The conversation had to do with her agent. She'd called him and told him what she thought of his tacky taste; and yet that evening she'd been up on the Strip only to see a fresh new billboard of a large scantily clad picture of her excerpted from a shampoo commercial a few years back. Her name and her agent's phone number were blocked out in bold five-foot letters below. I had missed it. She told me where it was, then shrugged and observed resignedly how everything was out of control. I asked her about this and got nothing for my effort.

"If your agent's embarrassing you," I told her, "get rid of him. That's all you have to do."

She shook her head. "There are other factors," she said quietly.

"Like what?"

She told me she had to think about it. Then, as if she'd just thought of something, she put her glass down abruptly and moved out of the room. I stood in the kitchen doorway and watched that walk of hers. It was like a mirage. I blinked, looked again, and she had disappeared in the short hall. I was getting mildewed in my soggy coat, so I took it off and put it on the back of a director's chair, then I leaned up against the sink counter and waited. The Glenlivet and the memory it inspired was warming me into a mood of quiet melancholy and charging it with a Byronic tinge of electric romance. I felt a sense of peace that was somehow unbearably intense. It was like her walk, moving and still and finally unsettling.

There were bathroom sounds, the toilet flushing, water running, quiet footsteps. I waited as the footsteps moved not toward me, but away. I sat down in the director's chair.

"Come here." Her voice, a peremptory whisper, echoed faintly, caressed and chilled me as it commanded.

I looked at the ice cubes in my empty glass and wondered whether I'd been doped. I shrugged and got up from the table and went down the short hall, turned with it, and found myself before the open door to a dark room. I couldn't see her but she was there. A flame flared, it was a lighter and she was holding it, then she placed it on a night table by the bed. The flame pulsed madly. She was on her back and the fur coat was spread out beneath her. She was fully dressed. I moved to the foot of the bed as she hiked up the long gown and let down her stockings.

I moved over and started kissing her. She pushed me off, but spread her legs and arched her back. I undid my belt.

She shook her head. "With our clothes on."

And so we had each other. She gave herself to me hard, bucking savagely, but her breath caught like mine had in the porno movie. It was a painful sound like she wanted to cry out but couldn't. Her nails dug into my back and she bucked harder. She wouldn't let me kiss her until I was about to come. The she raped me with her tongue. I could feel her stomach spasm. We came together as we were kissing for the first time.

I had no idea what time it was or how long this had taken, but it had seemed like less than a minute. We stayed still for a moment. I had my head buried in her shoulder, then I raised myself up on my arms and peered down at her face. It was like a death mask, the mouth serene, the eyes motionless. It flickered and pulsed at me in the odd light.

Her lips opened with invisible strings that kept the mouth unchanged in its expression. "All right," she said in a clear, normal speaking voice, "get out."

Her voice ran through me like a spike. Killing words said without the slightest trace of hurt or malice. It made sense but I didn't know why. Later, I had a feeling I'd get a better idea. For now, I stood up and zipped my pants. I left her alone there, without another look, and walked back out into the rain.

It was coming down harder.

The night was over.

12

"Why won't you let Jeeeesus be your friend? For *He* said—"

I turned off my clock radio and sat up with a groan. 7:30. Nothing like Brother John's Evangelical Prayer Hour to get a fella up and at 'em. I hadn't overslept in a year. I put on my flannel robe and woolen Mukluks, shuffled through the bathroom and kitchen, parted the beaded curtain and stepped into Petey's room. He wasn't there. Stanley wasn't there. The bed hadn't been slept in. I opened the kitchen door, shielded my eyes against the low sun, looked outside, then dragged myself around the house. Neither boy nor dog.

My nose was stuffed up. My head felt like an accordion. I tried to remember what I'd had to drink the last night and took two Tylenol with an Alka-Seltzer. I stripped down, climbed into the shower, turned the hot and cold all the way on, stood close to the nozzle, and let the water beat my head. After five minutes, I got out and put on fresh clothes. My corduroy sportscoat was damp and stretched out of shape, so I opted for my leather flight jacket. I put on my answer-phone, took a hanky, and walked out to the car. The sun slipped into hiding before I was half-way down the hill. It would be raining before noon.

Heading out west on Santa Monica Boulevard, car jockeys kept pace with me, idling and revving their souped up sports cars and hot rods and wanting to race me off the line at stoplights. Most were guys my age or older, wearing suits and ties. There was something pitifully comical about this. I was sick of the Ferrari already.

The Wild Oak School was on Little Santa Monica Boulevard, occupying the second floor above a row of ticky-tacky shops across the street from the Beverly Hills YMCA and the exclusive Friars Club. Wild Oak was an accredited alternative school for spoiled, foreign, or disabled kids, sometimes all three. From what I'd seen, they tended to be rich middle-easterners who spoke three words of English and spent most of their free time toying with money as if they were playing Monopoly; or local rich kids with movie star last names who didn't understand why they couldn't do whatever they wanted—they had the most outstanding behavior problems; black kids, or the ones without designer clothes and matching jogging shoes, specialized in learning disabilities and paid their tuition with the aid of state and federal grants. I'd never been impressed with the place, but since Petey had been labeled a behavior problem and a slow learner, I'd sent him here by process of elimination.

Gingerly, I opened the broken glass door and told the receptionist I wanted to see my kid. Petey had run away two times before and I'd found him at school eventually. He'd never ditched here and now I thought I knew why. I waited around, sitting with a lobbyful of current and prospective school parents. One was mocha colored with straight black hair that showed neatly from the sides and back of his tall white turban; another was an aging TV comedienne who had lately taken to endorsing cut-rate Kleenex; yet another was a stolid, heavy-set black lady with three darling little boys who were etching quaint lettering into the fiberglass chair seats with their key chains.

After five minutes of watching them, I got up and went down the hall as a recess bell rang and eighty or ninety kids came pouring out of the classrooms. I stopped a few of them, found out where Petey's classroom was, and went in through the open door. Kids were coming in and out, but five or six were scattered about on legless, tattered couches, either smoking or trying to snooze. Long sink-troughs lined the sidewalls, and large formica tables were grouped together in a work area behind the couches. Newspaper, and wet and dry clay, were strewn about here in great profusion. Pots, bowls, and unfired free-form sculptures were clustered on a table by a small, brick kiln lodged against the rear wall. Four or five other kids were standing around the work tables, talking as they toyed abstractedly with fresh hunks of clay. They all made a show of being cool and ignoring me as I looked around for Petey or the teacher. I waited for the passing and tardy bells until I realized that all of the classes were on different schedules. When the first bunch went back to class, this bunch and some others got out.

I followed the kids into the hall. No one I asked had any idea where Petey or their teacher might be. I walked back toward the reception area and thought I saw Petey's two girl friends coming out of a room down the hall. Angry now, I came back to the receptionist and demanded to see the principal. Principals are somewhat like agents or producers in the sense that they're always in conference. I waited all I could stand, then I barged into Doctor Strum's office.

Doctor Strum had nice legs for a principal. They were up on her desk. Her red, red nails matched her red, red lipstick. A Ritz cracker was in between the two and the Ritz box was on her lap. She took an angry bite out of the cracker, swung her legs off the desk top, and glared at me as she sat up.

"May I help you?" she asked with relaxed disdain.

Well, I told her how she could help me, and many other things besides, most of which had to do with my very critical opinion of how her school was run without much guidance, foresight, or reasonable authority. In return, roundaboutly, my ideas were bounced back at me as homespun neo-Nazi platitudes. Petey's teacher had a "very good reason" for not having been in the classroom; as far as my criticism that most of the ceramics work seemed to be centered around the construction of "bongs" or intricate hookah pipes, Doctor Strum contended that the drug problem would be worse were it not brought out into the open—and what the students did outside of school was only their own or their parents' responsibility. I was encouraged to withdraw my son from Wild Oak if I was not satisfied.

I wasn't getting anywhere. I stormed out as I had stormed in. Petey's little short-haired girl friend was standing on the sidewalk in front of Sam's car.

"What do you want?" I barked at her.

She stood her ground blandly, almost like a society matron who was too busy with the whole party to pay attention to a token, crass rube. "Is something wrong with Peter?"

"Yes, there might well be," I mocked. "For, you see, upon your parting, *Peter* took a solitary stroll; henceforth, he failed to return."

"He came over to my house," she said a bit loudly with a smirk.

"Where's that?"

She knitted her brows. "You're not gonna tell my parents?"

"Of course not," I coaxed.

She gave me her Beverly Hills address. Petey and the dog had made it over there about two-thirty. The little girl's bedroom was in a guest cottage out behind the main house. They had gone for a walk. Petey had talked about running away and asked her if she wanted to go with him. They were going to talk it over at school the next day.

I never would have gotten this out of her if she hadn't been worried. They'd been walking around Beverly Hills' small industrial warehouse district and Petey had decided to crash out in an unlocked storeroom.

I put her in the car and she directed me over to the warehouse and pointed out the storeroom. I zipped her back to the school, then returned. The Beverly Hills Post Office loading dock and a hamburger stand named Jack's were directly across the street. There were actually two warehouses, identical brick and corrugated aluminum structures that faced each other across a wide, empty rough gravel lot. Each had four storerooms, totalling about 1,000 square feet. I went up to the one Petey's girl friend had pointed out, slipped off the broken padlock, pulled the bolt, and swung up the light metal garage door: a gray concrete floor, a bare overhead bulb, and a big packing blanket balled up in the far corner.

I went over to the blanket and shook it out. There were white hairs on it. The thing seemed to have Stanley's smell. Petey could have been there, all right, but this was the only way I had of knowing; otherwise, the cold room was barren.

I came out and pulled down the door. Then I tried the locks on all the other storerooms, with no success. A small green trailer sat on cinder blocks at the rear of the lot. Dust-covered and faded, with cracked windows, I assumed it was abandoned, until I thought I saw some blinds move on the inside. I walked over and knocked on the door, then put my ear against it when nobody answered. Somebody was tip-toeing over the creaky floor. I knocked again, harder.

"I know you're in there," I called through the door.

No answer.

I'd have to do the talking. "I'm looking for my son," I said, "I have reason to believe he spent the night here in one of your warehouses."

The door swung open as I was finishing the sentence. A long-limbed, natty old man stood above me in the open door. He had silky white hair combed back off a narrow, sagging, anemic face. His shiny rimless glasses were squared off on the corners and went well with the flat rectangle of his red and white polka dot bowtie. His dark blue suit was double-breasted with shiny brass buttons, though his white shirt was yellowed and frayed at the cuffs and collar. His shoes, too, though nicely polished, were nicked and bowed with long wear. He twiddled a gold pencil between his first and second fingers and looked at me with an open, drooping jaw. His gray eyes were large and liquid. I had the feeling, even before he spoke, that we were intimates and he wanted to hug me like a long lost grandson.

"They must have called you first thing," he said softly.

I looked at him like he was crazy.

"They'll be here any minute," he went on mournfully.

"Have you seen my son?" I asked him. "He's a little short, thirteen, blond, long hair."

The old man reached into his pocket and came up with a pack of sugarless gum. "Would you like some?" he offered.

"No thanks. Could you please explain—have you seen him?"

He put the gum back into his pocket without taking a piece. "Yes, I found him."

"Where is he?"

"Please, won't you step in?"

He kept talking as I stepped up into the trailer. Something about how these warehouses were his son's property and he came by once a month to do some of the books, just to keep a hand in. He was trying to change the subject. To one side, the grimy linoleum was stacked with boxes; the other part was dusted clean with a small refrigerator and a speckled kitchen nook. Ledgers and cancelled checks were piled over the small table. A tiny portable reading lamp made a bright pool of light over a paper covered with neat columns of figures. The old man sat down in the far seat and motioned for me to join him.

"I saw you prowling around," he was saying. "You understand."

I must have appeared angry to him. He was apologizing. I shook my head. "No, I'm sorry."

"The police told me to be careful, so before you identified yourself—"

This nice little talk was leading somewhere I'd never imagined. The old man's careful soft voice was lulling me in an eerie, trance-like way. I swallowed and shook my head around, then I planted my hands on the table and leaned towards him.

"Show me where he is," I whispered like a dead man.

"I was instructed to keep the area closed off until they arrive. I'm sorry. They'll be here shortly."

My hands were gripping the edge of the table, shaking with strain. The lamp fell over. I could feel warmth across my stomach as the high-intensity bulb concentrated there. The old man's pallid face was shiny in the bad light. He looked away from me, then he got up and I followed him outside. We crossed the yard and approached the storeroom next to the one I'd searched. He took out a large key-ring, tried a couple of keys before he found the one he wanted and popped open the padlock. I reached over his hand, pushed the bolt, swung up the door, and rushed in.

A small form in black and white was lying over a white sheet at the back of the room.

"No."

I stopped, took deep breaths that didn't take, and moved the rest of the way, panting to catch oxygen. I fell to my knees, cupped my left hand around the small neck, and lifted it to look into a little boy's face I'd never seen before. He was nine or ten years old, smaller than Petey, with dark-blond, bowl-cut hair around a slightly chubby, roundish face. His eyes and lips were closed and he looked peaceful, but there was an unpleasant chemical odor about him. I put him down gently and plopped down on the floor with my back to him and both legs outspread. I saw red-black for a moment, but then I could breathe again. The oxygen rolled in, lapping my lungs with its easy tide. I let my head loll and went limp for a second like a rag doll.

"That's not him," I said finally, looking up at the spiffy old man.

We heard sirens then. I got up and followed the old man into the yard. Two Beverly Hills squad cars, with a uniformed team to each car, turned hard into the drive.

Their overhead lights were showy in the sunless cloud-cover. They ground toward us and rolled to a halt. Gravel sprayed out from under the lead car's front tires and nicked my ankles.

It was pretty routine. One of them questioned the old man, Mister Tenson; another questioned me, wanting to know what I'd been doing there. One of the guys in the back car remembered me from another encounter. He came up to me, snapping his fingers as he tried to recall my name. I gave it to him and it clicked. After that, they got much nicer. I made a few short, harmless quips about our mutual friend, Steifer, just to make sure they felt secure with me—for cops, as everybody knows, are a very clubby bunch: They belong and your problem is convincing them that you do.

Then I gave them the specifics. Petey hadn't come home and his little girl friend had last seen him here. I explained why I had reason to believe he'd spent the night. Print-people and the coroner were on the way, and I was told they'd make all the positive ID's. We left the old man and I followed them back to the station and had some coffee as they called around. Nothing came up right away which, I was told, was a good sign. They took my phone number and told me to go home—after the Captain, who'd been eavesdropping, came up to me, slapped my knee, and said heartily that so far we didn't have proof that my son had actually set foot onto the warehouse grounds and, even if he had, it didn't follow that his disappearance was necessarily linked to the body. Time, manner, and place of death for the little boy, a positive ID, the lab boys, etc., would give us a clearer picture of what we had. Lost, I nodded along. I knew only that I was scared. Petey had probably spent at least part of the night in a place where another boy had been found dead. I couldn't help thinking that there had to be a connection, besides, I didn't have any other leads.

"Go home, relax," he told me. "We'll tell ya soon as we know anything."

I didn't like it. It didn't feel right. Something was wrong and all of us could sense it. When I got up and put my jacket back on, I must have looked worried because the cop who had recognized me started talking too much instead of just signing off with a simple, "See ya around." I'd said that Petey had run away before. True. Two years ago, right after I'd adopted him, he'd split for two days—that had been when I wouldn't let him stay home for the whole World Series; then, a half a year later, three days, when I'd grounded him for not doing his chores. But I'd never experienced this panicky Mother Hen feeling before. Maybe I was getting older. My nerves were getting jumpy. I couldn't drink the way I used to without feeling it every once in a while.

More coffee and breakfast, that's what I needed. I thanked the boys for their time and walked outside. The sky made me very nervous. It was light, then dark, and the crisp air was too still. Shadows danced all over the place and prompted paranoid fantasies. Someone or something was behind me or hovering just above my head.

13

It was noon by the time I walked into Nate 'N' Al's Delicatessen and put my name in for a table. The small waiting area was jammed already and I was pushed up against the takeout counter by the door. I don't care if you're Joe Blow or the Shah of Iran, whether you have money or not has nothing to do with it: nine out of ten of them are either king or pilot fish, the haves and have-nots. Kings are the most bored people you'll ever see, pilots are the hungriest. Kingfish will stare at everyone around them as long as they can get away with it. They're always bored, restless, and prying with a sort of unfocused glaze in the eye that tells you they don't know what they're looking for. It's like they're walking around with fishbowls over their heads, not wanting you to see it as they try to find a way out of themselves. Pilots don't see this. They're too busy trying to attach themselves to kings; and pilots will stare at you forever, too, no matter what you look like, trying to figure out if you're king or pilot yourself. Either way, they want to know if they can use you. That's the way it is in crowded posh restaurants. You feel like you're being devoured. It can take a lot out of you; of course, if you're not depressed, it doesn't bother you. Sometimes, it can even be fun.

Right now, it wasn't. I turned to the take-out counter, ordered a pastrami on a kaiser roll and got out of there. I opened it up and ate some in the car, but I had no appetite. I passed the Queen of Babylon walking by the Tiffany Theater. She was wearing iridescent canary yellow spandex tights with black heels and a pair of red pasties with strings. I got indigestion just looking at her. My hangover came back full strength. Bob Hope's theme song rattled through my sodden brain: "Thanks for the memories . . . da da da da da da . . . da da da da da da . . ."

I downshifted and screamed up the canyon in seconds, stopping at the Country Store for a medicinal half-pint. The rain started lightly as I parked in front of my house. The sky had turned to slate, but at least it wasn't falling. Nothing was hovering over my head. It was just the rain, and the rain would go away.

My thoughts were turning simple on me. I needed that, though it would never work. You had to expect things to be complicated around here; otherwise, you belonged on a farm. You couldn't be in both places at the same time. I tugged on the bottle, trying to remember what a haystack looked like, cows, calves, and furrowed fields. They were only words now. I hadn't lived on a farm since I was seven years old, my grandfather's, because my folks had just busted up for the first time and my mother had left me out there. That had been the beginning of a long trail of "aunts," "uncles," Mister and Missus Johnsons, and Officer Rileys, from a summer idyll at Grandpa's to foster homes, orphanages, youth facilities, and the road. The road. Damn, it was a wonder I wasn't dead or in jail. But I wasn't, and, well, if the kid wanted to go the same route, he would—no matter what I thought about it. He'd survive. I had.

I took a few more swigs of firewater and watched the rain play over the windshield. I finished the sandwich, then I went into the house and played back the messages on my answerphone. Sam had called twice. Before and after, there were hang ups and no messages, all probably from Sam's office. Sounded like they were in a tizzy over there. Alfie Wilde's cold ears must have been turning warm.

I came out of the bathroom and moved over to turn off the tape.

"Somebody wants to talk to you—" I heard as I hit the cutoff button.

I backed up the tape and started it again.

"Somebody wants to talk to you." There was a pause, then: "Ben, it's me, Pete. These guys got me. Listen to what they say." The first voice took over again: "Hundred thousand dollars. . . . Dress him like a fuckin' millionaire, don't ya? . . . Don't ya?"

I winced, seeing Petey as a sitting duck in his fancy duds. A voice spoke in the background.

"Yeah, yeah," he told them. Then, into the receiver again: "One-zero-zero-zero-zero-zero by tomorrow evening. We'll call an' tell you where. Seven o'clock, be home . . . an' if you make a mistake . . ."

He hung up. I rewound the tape and played it back many times. Petey sounded a little too calm, but, considering he said so little, it was impossible to tell. The messenger had a high, fake, manic voice. It was filled with giddy cruelty, like a perverse Mickey Mouse. He enjoyed twisting the knife. The more I listened to him, the more he scared me. He sounded like he was barely under control.

I turned off the tape and sat there for a moment, not sure what to do. Then I picked up the phone, called the Operator and asked for the Beverly Hills Police. I hung up before it rang through. They already knew I suspected my son had been kidnapped. They'd trace it and call me if they discovered anything. I'd given them one of my wallet pictures of him. There was nothing else they needed and I didn't want them to tell me what to do. I had to handle this in my own way. I'd never forgive myself if something went wrong and I hadn't.

I sat there and tried to think. Finally, I called Information and got the number of the L.A. County Coroner's office.

"L.A. County Coroner's Investigations—Langsley speaking," said a tired sounding desk jockey.

"Gillis, Beverly Hills. Got anything on that little John Doe yet?"

I said it fast like I didn't have time for any bullshit and held my breath.

"What's the number?"

"I don't know. I haven't been back to the office. I'm callin' from a restaurant."

Pause, then: "Well, when it'd come in?"

"No more than an hour ago."

"Hold on . . . Yeah, they just brought it in—too early. That's one-fifty-four for your callback."

"Did you check?"

"I closed my eyes and pinned the tail on the donkey."

He was laughing as he cut me off. I made instant coffee and sat there staring at the phone, sweating like a pig as I tried to figure out what the hell I was going to do. I took off my flannel shirt, pulled on a T-shirt and sweated through that. I opened the kitchen door and watched the rain through the screen. Every ten minutes or so, it was coming down as hard as hail, playing my roof gutters like steel drums. Occasionally, there was some halfhearted thunder and lightning.

I didn't expect anything so soon, but I didn't know what else to do, so I called back, using the same approach but with the John Doe number this time. I was surprised when the desk jockey complimented me on my timing and asked me what color shirt he was wearing. I said I had no idea.

"What year, month, and day was I born on?" he persisted.

"I'm in a hurry," I told him.

"You're psychic," he said with phony drama.

"So?"

"Gillis, it's no fun down here. Don't you understand?"

I told him I understood in a way that implied I didn't have time for his problems.

"The boy's mother is sitting three feet away from me," he said, lowering his voice to a husky whisper.

"Are you kidding or what?" I asked impatiently.

"No. The father just came out and told her. I suppose you want names and all."

"Yeah," I sighed.

"Hold on."

I waited till the jerk came back on the line, gave me the kid's parents' names and address, and told me they'd have more later. I hung up hating the guy's guts, but it wasn't his fault, He had no idea that, for me, this was far from business as usual. How could he know? To him, I was Detective Gillis of the Beverly Hills Police Department, a bored, tired fella in a cheap double knit suit with a worried wife and two wild children, a gussied-up RV and a speedboat hitched to a trailer waiting in my mort-gaged backyard as I daydreamed over my next paid vacation and wondered both whether I'd make it and whether I cared. How could a bored and tired Coroner's desk jockey know I wasn't a bored and tired cop if I didn't tell him?

I felt sick. I went in the bathroom, leaned over the sink, stuck my finger down my throat and gagged, making an unsuccessful effort to throw up. A fantasized image of the little blond boy's father walking into the meat cooler and finding his pride and joy laid out on a stainless steel slab kept kicking at me from behind the eyes. My head was pulsing like a sonar scan. I could see the kid's innocent round cherubic face. I saw the father from behind. He wore a suit over broad shoulders that were crumbling under the force of his sobs. His hands, tied eternally, were folded before him and stayed out of sight. He was a helpless, dumb thing. He could do nothing. He was me.

14

No, not yet. I had to talk to him: Howard Green, 9785 Roxbury Drive, Beverly Hills 90210. David was the boy's name. It was 2:00 PM by the time I arrived at their apartment on the poor end of Beverly Hills. Roxbury Park, with its bowling greens, little league fields, and tennis courts, was across the street, getting washed clean in the downpour. A tall, trim, gray-haired jogger, wearing a blue nylon sweatsuit, slogged by me on the sidewalk. I should have found this amusing, but today, like everything else, it seemed a little odd. For no apparent reason, erratic drivers alternately speeded and lurched at a crawl. These people weren't accustomed to playing second fiddle to nature. I'd been leaning on the Ferrari's snobbish, brassy horn all the way from Hollywood and my whitened knuckles were clamped down over the little steering wheel. I pried them loose and got out of the car.

The Greens' home was a handsome duplex, beige with brown shutters and a red tile roof. The hedges and ferns were trimmed and layered like jade plants, the signature of a meticulous Japanese gardener. Colorful ceramic tiles outlined the arch of the front door. I brushed my stringy, wet hair back, turned up the collar on the standard khaki trenchcoat I'd worn for effect, and rang the bell.

The door opened before I released my finger; thus the lower second chime clanged off as a small, slight young man held onto the inside door knob and looked at me as if he'd been expecting someone else. He had tightly curled, brown gray hair that he wore bushy with cuffed corduroy pants, penny loafers, and a light blue button-down oxford shirt. His eyes were a misty blue behind thick lenses in oval tortoiseshell frames set over a long, slightly aquiline nose. His brows bunched quizzically and I felt he was hoping, desperately against all logic, that I was some celestial delivery boy here to undo what could not be undone.

The quizzical look turned into a frown. "I'm sorry, whatever you want, we can't talk now."

The form of a petite pregnant woman had appeared in the background. "I'm not selling anything, Mister Green," I tried to convince him. "May I talk to you for a minute? It's important."

"For God's sake, Howard," the woman interceded, "close the door."

She didn't sound shrewish. She was genuinely frightened and I thought I understood. There was a terrible silence after this. A wall of rain pelted the cement walk behind my back, cutting off the zone of quiet a few feet away, but everything in front of me cried of mute, palpable grief. I'd been planning on impersonating a police officer or detective with these people, but now I knew I wouldn't be able to bring it off. Green started to close the door.

I put my foot inside. "I know what you're going through," I said quickly. "I know you just lost your son. My boy's just been kidnapped. I was hoping you could help me."

The door was jammed against my instep. It opened slightly and two overlarge Keene-ish brown eyes in a plain, pale, studious small face peered out at me. "Who are you?" her strained voice quavered. "How did you know who we are?"

"I'm Ben Crandel," I told her. "I was there when the police found your son's body. I impersonated a police officer and called the County Coroner's office to find out where you lived. If you'll let me in, I'll explain the rest of it."

The door opened. I walked into what looked like a student apartment, clean but spartan with a worn, over-stuffed couch, large throw cushions on the floor, and board and brick bookcases set about the room. At a glance, the big titles seemed to spell out sociology and education. Mrs. Green offered coffee, then left the livingroom before I answered either way. I could hear her crying in the kitchen. Her husband excused himself and went after her. The crying died down. He returned alone.

"She's a good person," he said abstractedly. "She didn't need this."

Without a sound, he started crying. The tears curved around the inside of his glasses and rolled down the sides of his nose. I sat there and watched him. It was one of the most unpleasant experiences of my life. The only thing I could do was to wait for him to regain his composure and hope he would start talking. He took off the glasses, wiped them on his shirttail, and set them back on without going over his eyes or face. I offered him my handkerchief but he didn't hear me.

"Your son's body has been kidnapped," he began finally.

His choice of words and how they added up piqued me, but I thought he was too upset to be thinking clearly.

"That's right," I said.

"How much do they want for it?" he asked me.

I stopped and looked at him. He was sitting in an old oak rocker across from the couch, waiting for my answer. We seemed to be talking apples and oranges. "My boy's alive," I said.

He sat forward, put his chin in his hands, and propped an elbow on each of his knees. "Your son wasn't dead?" he asked me.

"I don't get what you mean."

"I'm talking about body ransoming, 'body heisting,' the police called it," he started to explain, stopping as his voice weakened.

"Take your time," I encouraged him.

He nodded. I got up, went to the kitchen, and brought him a glass of water. "Thank you," he said after a swallow. "Needless to say, this is painful business. Let me explain. My wife and I are high school teachers. We know the L A. school system, so we moved to Beverly Hills so David could go to school here. The best, only the best. We pay a fortune for this apartment, but it's a good school, good area, right across from the park— what else could we ask for?"

A car speeded by outside, splashing water as it planed its way through the rain. Green jumped to his feet. "That, though, we didn't know about," he yelled, turning around and gesticulating toward his front window. "We didn't know what morons drive around here—rushing—where are they rushing to, Saks, I. Magnin's?" He paused, breathing hard, then came back to his chair and sat down. "I've been through this," he said quietly. "Everybody thinks they own the road when they're behind their steering wheel. My son was hit on his bicycle, riding in the street. Maybe he darted out, I don't know. It doesn't matter. Broke his neck—this is two days ago. Yesterday, the day of his funeral, we got a phone call. This guy wanted five hundred thousand dollars for David's body."

Needlessly, I asked him about the voice. It was the same one. He lapsed off for a moment. I asked him what he did.

"What would you do?!" he demanded.

"I wouldn't know," I admitted.

"Obviously," he said angrily, "they thought we were royalty. You can see we're not royalty." He gestured toward the room and its furnishings. "Besides, we're not exactly religious, if you know what I mean. David is gone. Giving his body a proper burial doesn't mean very much to me—in fact, it means nothing. Is that going to bring him back?!" He paused, leaned forward again, and put his chin in his hands. "It was the aggravation. We called the funeral people, they called the police, we called the police. All day yesterday, this creep kept calling us. Finally, I offered him two thousand dollars, half of our savings. I was supposed to meet him for an exchange halfway out in the desert. I went and no one was there."

"Your ante wasn't high enough."

"I suppose not."

"Have there been any other victims like yourself?"

"I don't know. I think so. Are you asking me because you plan to look into it?"

I studied his vague eyes, wondering what he wanted

me to say. I needed more information out of him and I was willing to say whatever I had to in order to get it.

"Of course you're going to," he said for me, his face coloring for a moment. "What's wrong with me?"

He'd forgotten momentarily what my reasons were for being so inquisitive. I smiled meekly as he trotted out everything he could to help me and wrote down the name and address of the mortuary, his funeral director, and the police names he could remember. Without being asked, he volunteered his silence on the whole matter as it concerned me, then got up and walked me to the door, saying that he'd explain it to his wife when she was feeling better.

He flicked a finger toward the scratch paper as I put it into my pocket. "Our phone number's at the bottom," he told me. "Call us, please."

We shook hands, he wished me luck, and I walked back into the rain.

15

"Detective Gillis, Beverly Hills Police Department. Is Mister Johnson in?"

I reached into the inside pocket of my trenchcoat, extracted my billfold, and flashed one of my library cards in the general direction of a middle-aged woman doing battle against the encroachment of senior citizenship in an excruciating powder blue, belted wool shift stretching at all its midseams and sending pressure on upward that seemed to explain her excessive rouge and lipstick widened lips. Her modest chest equipment was showcased in a pointy push-up bra and a frosted beehive hairdo spiralled skyward from her head. She looked like a pin could pop her and send her flying around the room.

She stopped typing and looked at my billfold without really looking. "I'm sorry," she apologized in a tobacco coarsened, pleasant voice, "but Mister Johnson is very busy. Is it possible you could return tomorrow morning?"

She was businesslike, yet friendly in a matronly way that jibbed with her retired gun moll image. "We have a few more questions," I said vaguely, by way of explanation.

She reached for a Kent, lit up, and exhaled her slight displeasure. "There have been so many distractions because of this . . . mishap," she sighed, looking perplexed at losing the train of her thought. "It's just become rather difficult to carry on with the present business," she finished off after another long drag.

"We have some new information," I said politely. "If Mister Johnson is here, I'm afraid I'll have to ask that you let me see him."

She nodded resignedly and pushed the button on her intercom without another word. "Bill, I know you said not to bother you, but the police are here again," she told the box with her soft, raspy voice.

"Send them in," replied a youngish sounding voice.

I thanked the secretary, told her I hoped I hadn't gotten her into trouble, and went into the inner office. Common among American mortuaries, its pseudo-Tudor motifs strived for the same staid, time-tested, august and dour solemnity as the trimmings on the exterior facade. Outside, the Johnson Funeral Home had the basic threefold combination of slanted roofs, snaking, crisscrossed support timbers, and dark leaded windows; inside, the director's office was lined with smooth dark oak to a white plaster ceiling covered with evenly spaced roughhewn beams. The effect was sort of like being in a pit with bars over your head.

A young man in his early twenties sat before me at an oversized Regency desk. Two large wing chairs in crushed red velvet squatted before it. Five or six plaques from various societies and schools of Mortuary Science decorated the panelling behind his high-backed, studded leather chair. Trade journals, *Professional Embalmer, Cemetarian*, etc., faced me over the edge of the desk. On one of them, a squat, hairless fellow, featured embalmer of the month, I supposed, sat behind a desk much like this one and smiled with restrained dignity for the big pic. He was night and day compared to the tall kid who stood up, extending the long arm of a basketball jock, and shook my hand like he was congratulating me on a good play. He wore baggy low-waisted blue jeans and a yellow armed baseball undershirt. The *L.A. Times* and *Examiner* sports pages were lying to the side next to a fat copy of the latest *Playboy*. A textbook was open in front of him. He'd been working on it with a transparent yellow marker.

"Jeff Gillis."

"Bill Johnson . . . Boards coming up," he said, gesturing toward the book, then slamming it shut with disdain.

We sat down. He kept talking without much coaching. As it turned out, the kid's old man had kicked off a half-year ago and he was running the family business until they were ready to sell it. He was a med student and he depended upon the woman outside, Roberta, to keep it all going. She'd been around as long as he could remember. I got him to hand me all of this by pretending I knew it already but was just going over old ground to see if I'd missed anything, which also implied that I was trying to trip him up. That got him serious, but he wasn't too nervous. He seemed to be playing it straight. On the hope that I was still one step ahead of the cops, I told him that we'd found the Green boy and asked for his list again of the others.

"It's just Levotsky and Crane," he said, looking at me

as if I should have known. He chewed on his wispy moustache and looked aside at his textbook.

"They've kidnapped a live one," I said, straining to appear disinterested.

A strand of his lanky black hair fell over one eye. He blew it off his face like a kid would do and gestured toward me with the palms of his hands. "What do you want me to do?" he asked.

"I'm trying to set some fire under you," I told him. "Think. Is there anything you might have forgotten? Before, you mentioned that employee . . ."

"Ted Aikens. I told you guys a million times."

"I want you to describe him again," I urged him. "Try to forget what you told us yesterday or the day before. Picture him."

He closed his eyes as he described the kidnapper to me. "Five-eight, five-nine, one-sixty, one-seventy pounds. Short brown hair, small face, muscular in the chest and arms."

"That's what you said before," I estimated.

He opened his eyes. "Well, that's how I see him," he insisted.

"I'll give you a star for consistency," I tried to joke. "Now, he worked here for how long?"

"One month."

"In what capacity?"

"As I said, driver."

"His disposition?"

"Nice. Kind of shy, well mannered."

"No problems of any kind."

"None."

"Just very polite and he skipped."

"That's right," came his chipper voice, working to maintain his patience.

"OK," I said summarily. "I guess it's up to us to do our

homework now." I sneezed, took out my hanky, and wiped my runny nose.

Young Johnson studied me a moment, then he scribbled something on his scratchpad and handed it across the desk. "Chlortrimeton," he said. "It's non-prescription, good stuff."

I looked at the paper. The script heading said *Johnson Funeral Home, serving Westwood since 1926.* I had to laugh. "A prescription from a future doctor on his family's funeral home stationery. Are you sure you're sincere?"

Young Johnson didn't take it as a joke. He swiveled in his chair, turning toward the leaded window. "This has been an embarrassment to me my whole life," he said emptily.

Which was probably why he wanted to be a doctor. It was as far away as he could get from following in his father's footsteps. Ordinarily, I would have picked up on a remark like that and been curious to know more about what it had been like growing up as a mortician's son, but now I had something much more important to worry about.

Still, as I walked out onto Westwood Boulevard, I couldn't help wondering whether young Johnson would go all the way in exorcising his inheritance. Obstetrics, I thought, would be perfect.

16

My man Gillis was acquitting himself rather well. I felt confident he'd stand up for me again in a pinch if I needed to make use of him, but in a couple of hours or so I'd probably do well to change his name. I'd come close to getting what I wanted from Johnson junior, but I'd been wary of asking too much about what I was already supposed to know. I needed addresses for the two corpses and the driver. If I had to, I was going to call Johnson back and mumble something about a departmental foul-up to try to get my information. That would ring about as true as Ethel Merman's singing.

I rushed up Westwood Boulevard and headed straight for the UCLA Law Library where they keep the daily papers before transferring them to microfilm. I filled out a request card for all the papers from the last two weeks and made eyes with the wall clock until they arrived. Then I sat down at one of the long tables and irritated a number of students as I crackled the pages going through to scan the Death Notices in each daily local news section. Gerome Levotsky was listed under last Tuesday; the boy, David Green, and Julius Crane were under Wednesday. Levotsky had been the "beloved husband of the late Sylvia Levotsky; loving father of Herman A. Levotsky—services and interment private." The private services and interment were odd, I thought. David Green's parents had scheduled services for "Thursday, 12 noon at Hillside Memorial Chapel. Johnson Funeral Home, Directors." And Julius Crane who had been the "Beloved husband of Mrs. Miriam Crane; devoted father of Charlene and James," was scheduled for "Rosary, Thursday, 7 PM at Johnson Funeral Home, Westwood. Funeral Mass Friday, 10 AM at St. Mary Magdalen Chapel, Camarillo. Interment Friday, 3 PM in Inglewood Park Cemetery."

I turned in the papers, found a public phone down the hall, and called Information. There was nothing in all of L.A. for either Levotsky or Crane, but Ted Aikens, the driver for the funeral home, was listed. This was a big lucky stroke, but I didn't want to go too fast. I got his West Hollywood address, hung up, and stood there, wiping my nose and feeling bothered by something I couldn't put a finger on. Then it clicked.

I walked out into the rain and sloshed across campus to the Cinema Library. By the time I walked into the main building, my wingtips were soggy enough to hang out on a line and my nose had taken on a will of its own. My throat felt raw when I swallowed. I tried to ignore all of this and ran up the stairs to the library. I passed students who looked barely older than Petey, found my way in and rushed to the "Who's Who" books, then switched to Leslie Halliwell's *Filmgoer's Companion:*

"Wilde, Alfie (1915–) (Herman Alfred Levotsky) Austro-Hungarian writer-director, in Hollywood more or less from 1935. At his height, a specialist in searing comedy and hardedged drama drawn straight from the daily headlines, although lately he has landlocked his talent with dull, lugubrious fare."

Alfie Wilde had fallen off the wagon and been obsessed with ghosts and fathers on the day we met, the day he committed suicide. I knew nothing about the man's roots or the intricacies of his personal life, but obviously there had been unresolved conflicts and difficulties. He had said the ghosts could not be calmed and that, in the case of another disturbed patient, it was necessary to kill the parent in order to be free, although there was also a danger of killing or obliterating the self in the process. All of this had been a long-winded, uphill struggle with guilt. And it had finally gotten the best of him. I surmised that Alfie had probably refused to pay ransom for his father's corpse and the bodynappers had worked on him to help him change his mind. I could just see them propping the body up outside Alfie's bedroom window. Some scheme like that. The hook hadn't taken, at least not right away.

Petey and I had stood at the edge of the La Brea Tar Pits as they dredged out the remains of a little old man who, we believed, had never touched our lives. Then, he hadn't. Now, he had, not him exactly, but somebody who had been around him.

I could see the tar pit. My life seemed to be falling into that pattern—a bottomless pit with a false bottom. Distant things were close by. I just couldn't make them out. It was all fraught with a maddening elusiveness.

"Sir, may I help you?"

I was standing at the front counter. Two film students were behind me and the librarian was waiting for me to ask a question or move ahead. I closed my book and turned around. The second kid in line was ready to check out an old Alfie Wilde screenplay. I smiled and got out of there before I screamed.

17

I went home and called the police to find out whether they were ahead or behind me. But they wouldn't tell me any of their deep, dark secrets, so I played hard-to-get on my end, too. I called the Coroner's office to confirm my hunch about Alfie Wilde's father being the cast-off baggage dumped into the La Brea Tar Pits. Then I took off the soggy wingtips, changed my socks, pants, and shirt. I got up on the kitchen chair, took a shoebox down out of the cupboard above my refrigerator. I made myself a cup of instant, flicked on the electric wall-heater in the bathroom, and hung my raincoat from a towel rack a few inches away; then I came back into the kitchen, sat down at the table, sipped on the cup of coffee, and stared at the box.

I took a few deep breaths, then I opened it and took

out a heavy object wrapped in a greasy rag. I took the rag off and gawked at my Stainless Chief Special snubnose .38, Smith and Wesson Model 60. Guns. Yeah, they seem crude and superfluous—until something happens to you; then you decide you need one. It's no big deal, really. You don't agonize over it. You get in your car, drive to your local sporting goods store, and let the salesman talk you into the top of the line. You learn how to use it, then you stow it away and pretend to forget it exists. But you don't. If you're the sensitive sort, you begin to feel guilty for being paranoid and not trusting in the innate goodness of your fellow man; in your heart, you know you want it and when you hear the news, you're just positive that it's only a matter of time until we all don double six-guns to take a walk around the block.

Bang-bang, the thing didn't look real to me. I'd fired it probably a total of a hundred and fifty times in three sessions on a practice range and hadn't looked at it for over a year. It gave me the creeps. Fuck the bang-bang, this damn thing was such a toy that both of my hands were shaking as I cradled it in my palms. It was the situation, not the gun, that was unreal. I couldn't believe that Petey was gone, and I was planning to use this thing to get him back.

I opened the cylinder, checked to make sure it was unloaded, then I took the cleaning rod brush, dipped it in Hoppe's Nitro Powder Solvent, and cleaned out the bore. I put cleaning patches over the rod and pushed them through, did the same thing with the cylinder and all five chambers, then switched to an old toothbrush to go over the breachface, top-straps, and the interior of the frame. Finally, I used Triflon to oil the yoke and below the firing pin. After that, I went into the bedroom, lifted my nightstand, and picked up a box of Winchester lead hollow-point, semi-wad cutter bullets from underneath. I loaded the gun, clicked the safety, and stuck it in my pants. I pocketed the Winchesters along with a fresh hanky, put on a pair of jogging shoes, stretched my leather jacket over my gut and zipped up. Then I grabbed the wingtips and trenchcoat and hustled out to the car, feeling a little afraid of myself. I knew I wanted to kill somebody, and what frightened me was that I was justified, I had a real good reason. I let it drive me down the canyon like a bat out of hell. People honked and blinked their brights through the sodden gray day. That didn't bother me as long as they stayed out of my way, but I realized I was attracting too much attention. After all, I was driving someone else's expensive car and packing a gun, besides. I had to be careful.

After turning eastward on Sunset, I slowed to a canter, making my way past Highland to Wilcox. Aikens' place was close to Santa Monica Boulevard. It was a large, four-layered box with alternating blocks of brown and white gold-flecked stucco setting off each story. It looked like the design concept had been inspired by an upended milk carton. I put the extra shells in the glove box, locked it, and stepped out into a puddle that went halfway up my shins. The fucking rain. Nothing, nothing in this city takes moderation into consideration. It's either dull as hell or the shit completely hits the fan. Tepid or it comes on like a goddamn monsoon. L.A. doesn't know how to drizzle or rain lightly. Like a public transit system or the theater, it just wouldn't fit here.

I wasn't tense. I knew Aikens wouldn't be around. After knocking on his door and seeing the place was cleaned out, I went to the Manager's apartment, rang repeatedly and waited patiently as you must for most apartment managers who are always home and hiding, hoping you'll change your mind and try to fix the drain yourself. I ignored my sore thumb and persisted until the whining, despondent duet of the soap opera couple cranked down a notch and I was rewarded for my labors by the presence of a Broderick Crawford lookalike with a wine-vat belly, three chins, and enough jowls for a litter of bloodhounds. Opening the door fanned out the odor of cigar stubs and rancid bacon grease. His undersized torn silk kimono had been taken off a dead geisha doll and I felt awkward looking at his prodigious unclothed girth. Hairless legs stopped at his yellowed briefs which sprouted a little fan of hair that encircled his navel and stopped before a chest that was breasty, albeit hairless. I wondered whether all of this might have something to do with personal habits better left undisclosed. I did my best to smile, introduced myself as Aikens' old roommate, and asked him if he might have any inkling whatsoever as to my long lost buddy's present whereabouts.

Broderick told me to wait a minute, disappeared, then returned wearing some pince nez bifocals for what reason I knew not. He spoke with a resonant stage voice full of subtle nuances and pregnant starts and pauses. Before I knew it, he'd put a beer in my hand, I was sitting on an ugly Danish modern sofa, and he was showing me pictures of his dead cat. I noticed then that the one-room apartment smelled of cat piss. I've never had any use for cats, but I played along.

"Yeah, sure, I know what you mean."

I said it an easy ten times and finally went out on a limb and pretended to confess that I'd just lost my very own Siamese and was trying not to dwell on it. He told me I was right and then when I asked him about Aikens, he gave me another guy's name and apartment number out across the way at the rear of the building.

I thanked the man and suggested that he find himself

another cat. I left the beer and heard him crank up the soap opera as I walked down the outside hall.

I rang the tenant's bell, knocked, and got nothing. Somebody touched me on the shoulder.

"Try him about seven or eight."

The low voice had shifted into deep honey. He didn't have to say anything. I knew what this was about. "OK," I nodded, backing off.

"Come by if you feel like it. We could have another . . . beer."

"Why, sure, maybe. Why not?"

What else could I say to the guy? Christ, when I came back, the thing to do was to bring him another cat. That might help him keep his hands to himself.

18

I called Julius Crane's daughter from a gas station. Thanks to my nose being glued shut, my voice took on a doleful, grief-stricken quality that set just the right mood when I came on as a "business acquaintance" who had just received the unfortunate news through a mutual friend. Charlene put us on a chummy standing right off the bat by insisting that I call her Char. In no uncertain terms, she proceeded to tell me that she remembered me well from her parents' last Christmas party. Wasn't I in insurance? Why, of course. I asked her how she was getting on and found out she'd been recently divorced. Presently, she was attending real estate school after having completed graduate studies in art history. She was extremely apologetic about this, so I gave it my all to convince her I understood. I got daddy's phone number and address, including directions, before she asked me what my favorite painting was. I told her "Whistler's Mother," but she was quite serious about her art and didn't think I was being funny. That killed our chances for a successful marriage.

Crane's house was on Tower Road off Benedict Canyon, in between Sunset and Mulholland Drive. I put on my Detective Gillis get-up and drove over. Coming west on Sunset, you took a right on Benedict Canyon in front of the Beverly Hills Hotel and curved up through two long lights, making a soft right and quick sharp left onto Tower. It was easy to miss, but the homes sure weren't. Crane's fit in with all the rest. It was a large squat two-story Spanish mission styled structure that interwove art deco influences into the standard heavy stucco and roof-tile look. The huge front doorway was a series of six or seven concentric white rectangles that receded toward a glass door covered with ornate flowering grillwork.

I had the feeling I should have been wearing a rainhat. There was something irresponsible and amateurish about a detective walking around with a bare wet head. Rationalizing that, outside of TV, there aren't any hard and fast rules for appropriate plainclothes apparel, I rang the bell. A pretty young black woman in a plain white maid's uniform opened the door. Mrs. Crane was right behind her and, as far as my attire, she couldn't have cared less. She was totally juiced. I could smell the haze of alcohol that followed her from five feet away.

Before I could give my fake name or purpose, she came forward and wrapped her arms around my back. "Another friend of Julius. So nice of you to come. Char just called me. Come in, come in."

No need for Gillis. This was set for smoother going than I'd planned. "Thank you."

Mrs. Miriam Crane stopped bear-hugging me and led me through the long-mirrored entry into a living room that had been built for entertaining. Lush chrome-silver mohair couches lined most of the wall space that wasn't interrupted by the large parabolic shaped windows that either looked out to the rich front oval clover lawn before the drive or framed a bougainvillaea strewn courtyard with a large modern bronze fountain. The courtyard was protected by a large glasshouse ceiling that made a racket as the rain punched away at it. The fountain, I realized, was lit from the bottom of the pool. It was a tall gleaming tepee made of wiry looking poles. The water trickled from the top where they crossed and travelled their length dazzlingly, making a shiny ring as it slapped into the pool at the tepee's base. It was hard to take your eye off it. There were large canvases which, aside from what Char Crane probably thought of me, I would have enjoyed having the time to eyeball. Miriam Crane's short heels were clacking over the dark parquet that wasn't covered by an Oriental throw rug that must have taken a million hands a dynasty or two to finish.

Miriam walked me up to a glass-and-chrome bar, sat me down on a leather high stool, let go of me, and went behind. It felt lonely. There were nine other empty seats curving away on either side of me. Mrs. Crane checked herself in the back mirror and turned to me looking displeased with what she'd seen. A frosted glass etched frieze of mermaid girls, fawns, and exotic flowers was affixed to the mirror, and the sight of this woman's blotchy, hollow-eyed, and haggard face superimposed over the sprightly gaiety presented an unsightly contrast. Physically, Mrs. Crane was the sort of woman that people call handsome. She had a short, blocky figure, her hands were too large, her ankles too thick. Still, she had a girlish dignity about her. Even drunk, she carried herself with brisk, bouncy confidence. Her skin looked coarse without make up, but she didn't look like she felt like wearing any. Her little tweedy suit was neat, her green blue eyes were glassy, and her busy mouth was struggling against the vengeance of close, painful memories. She wasn't getting a damn bit of pleasure out of the alcohol, I could see that. An alky would have showed less. They can't help it. Their finer feelings are more deeply buried. She turned around again, putting herself among the mermaids.

"Ugh, I could die," she said. "I could die." Nervously, she patted her blowzy hairdo. Her long nails pulled the unkempt bird's nest farther apart.

I didn't know what to say to her. Abruptly, she shifted tacks, told me to take off my coat, and asked what I'd like to drink. I told her anything. She poured a tall glass full of Scotch and set it before me on the mirrored bar top.

"Ugh," she apologized, gesturing toward the glass with a long nail. "Here," she said, trying to take it back. "I forgot the ice."

"It's all right," I said, lifting it.

She poured herself the same thing, put it out next to mine, then folded her arms over the counter in front of me, dropped her head, and started sobbing. My drink spilled, but I caught the glass before it toppled over, saving some, and pushed both glasses to the side. I used my hand as a mop and swept most of the liquor over toward the sink side of the bar. Before I had finished, one of Mrs. Crane's hands appeared, groping the counter top for her drink while she kept her head down. I handed it to her.

She looked up, said, "I'm sorry," then she drank most of the glass.

I knew she'd pass out in another five or ten minutes. I had to talk to her fast. "I think you'd better sit down," I told her.

"Thank you," she said, coming out from behind the bar.

We walked over to the mohair couch in the far corner and sat down. She had lost her graceful carriage. I crossed a leg and played with the laces on one of my wet shoes, she slouched against the couchback, waiting to be ushered into oblivion. I took out my handkerchief and blew my nose. She sat up, then started to slouch again.

"It must be very difficult," I began.

The maid walked by in the hall. "Is that the doctor?" she asked.

"I don't think so."

She slouched back, dropping down a bit, and letting her legs bow open. "I need to sleep," she said quietly.

I didn't want to pounce on her raw and open wounds, but I had to; so, gratingly, I raised my voice and gave it a prodding tone. "It was bad enough already, wasn't it?"

"Terrible. I could die."

"I know. First you lose Julius, and, if that isn't bad enough, these . . . hooligans, these—"

"*Meshuggeners.*"

Yiddish? I hadn't expected that. Johnson Funeral Home wasn't a Jewish establishment. "*Meshuggeners,* that's right," I encouraged. "They take Julius. My God, I'm not exactly a part of your generation, but I wonder what the world is coming to lately when people like this are loose in the street."

"Ugh," she said, slouching lower.

"Don't you wonder, Missus Crane?"

"Ugh."

"Missus Crane?"

She sat up a little, her heavy eyes opened slightly, and she gave me a look like it was very early in the morning. "What are you yelling about?"

"It just gets me upset. I'm sorry," I said lamely.

She shook her head and frowned at me like she was looking at the class dunce. "Julius and I were married for thirty-seven years. Do you honestly think I care about his body?" She gave her shoulders a little shrug and gestured with the palms of her hands. "You don't know me," she went on, frowning again as she seemed to be trying to recall who I was. "He had so many business acquaintances. You all loved him. He was a fair man and a man of the family. He never messed around —not to my knowledge. He was Catholic, I was Jewish. He said that made a good mix—we could share our religious guilt together. What a charmer. When he dies, his sister wants a Christian funeral: so, you know what I say? Give her a Christian funeral. If it'll make her happy, it's all right by me. You understand me?"

"Sure, of course."

"Ugh." She started to doze off again, then her eyes opened to slits. "You know," she said, "you really *feel* Jewish when you're around people who are so . . . so *goyish*."

"What did you tell them when they wanted to sell Julius to you?"

Quickly, she sat up and leaned toward me, clenching her little fists. The glaze in her eyes had ignited into fire upon water. "And what makes you so curious, if I might ask?"

"We were just talking."

"It seems to me you were asking the questions, I was giving the answers. You're his sister's son, aren't you?"

"No, no, of course not."

She got to her feet. "You big weasel, I'll tell you what I said—but wait a minute; let me ask you this: having in my possession a dead, shrivelled body rotted away of cancer, is that going to bring back someone I love?! You morons!! What are you living for—to be dead?! If there's a heaven, he's there already, I can assure you."

"I'm sorry. I didn't mean—"

"She can have her masses, smashes if *she* pays for it. If she wants Julius back, *she* can buy him—understand? It hurts me, sure it does—but do you think I'm going to reward these . . . sick hoodlums when I don't have to? Let *her* if it's so goddamn important to her. She has the money—or did she already give it all to the Vatican? Did she?!"

"Missus Crane, I'm not related to—"

She interrupted, ticking off a numbered list on the fingers of her left hand. "One, I didn't meet with them; two, I didn't talk with them; three, I don't care what *she* thinks of me; four, I don't care what you think of me; five—"

She keeled over. I caught her and laid her out on the couch. I was getting into the Ferrari when a white Mercedes coupe came up the drive from behind me and parked to my right. I rolled down the rain-fogged window on the passenger side and watched a small man in a black rain slicker and shiny rubbers carry a plastic-wrapped black bag up the front steps.

The patient was resting. I felt like telling him he could leave his pills with me. Mrs. Crane's problems were ancient history. It was my headache now.

19

Musso and Frank's is the only class restaurant in town that has a counter and condones the lone wolf. You get your very own individual tablecloth that circumscribes and anchors the borders of your pride in case somebody you know sees you and walks up because they think you don't like being by yourself. I had a salad with oily roquefort dressing and liver sautéed with onions without incident, swallowed two cups of coffee, then went out and paced Hollyweird Boulevard, rubbing elbows with a nice crowd of Friday night juice heads, PCP freaks, bikers, runaways, and moviegoers tracking down the latest and greatest sex and violence. We were folks who seemed to have nothing to lose by getting soaked in the rain. Dry, wet, what did it matter? All of us were looking for something that had nothing to do with the weather: dope, juice, movies, boys, girls, money—maybe all of it.

Cruise and hang out, take it slow. Somehow, it would come to you if you didn't ask too loudly. Cops have good ears. You had to wait quietly.

No, I didn't have time for that. I took a look at the books on the outside remainder table under the awning in front of Pickwick Bookstore, then got in the Ferrari and drove back to Aikens' apartment building. Broderick's porchlight was on and so was Aikens' friend's across the way. I put my hands in my trenchcoat pockets and clicked off the safety, then I rang the bell. Blue TV light came through the drapes along with some rollicking canned laughter. I gave up ringing and pounded a few times.

"Yeah!" somebody yelled from behind the door.

Instead of yelling back and generating a commotion through the rest of the building, I kept knocking and waited. It worked. The door swung open toward the inside and a tall, lanky, swarthy guy glared at me from behind his screen and rubbed the motherfucker goatee running straight down the middle of his chin. He was barefoot in a pair of red flannel pajamas with white piping. He had big feet, a long, large head, a thin-lipped cynical mouth, and dark, beady eyes. I thought he might bite me.

"Yeah?" he growled.

The laughtrack continued inside. A big bar of light billowed out from around the guy's shoulders. I shifted my gaze and saw his image on a four foot square screen. He'd been watching himself on one of those home entertainment video tape gizmos. On tape, he was up on stage telling jokes and getting laughs.

"Sorry to bother you," I began, then snapped my fingers, feigning recognition. "Say, weren't you at the Comedy Store the other night?"

"No."

"I've seen you somewhere," I smiled.

"That's fascinating," he smirked, starting to close the door.

"Hey, can we talk for just a minute?"

"What do you want?"

"I'm an old roommate of Ted Aikens. I was wondering—"

"Were you his wife?"

"No."

"He was married for ten years. At least that's what he told me."

"This was before that."

"You musta been real good friends."

"Yeah, we were. Is anything wrong with that?"

"Not that I can think of. Hope ya find him."

He went back to closing the door. I unlatched the screen and met the door with my shoulder. "What the hell's wrong with you?" I demanded.

"Do you mind?"

"I thought you might have an idea how I might get ahold of my old buddy and you slam your door in my face. Lousy stand-up comedy, if you ask me."

"OK, I'll call the police," he snarled, batting his thick brows down at the wrinkles bunching over the bridge of a long, bony finger of a nose.

"Christ," I heaved out, ramming with my shoulder. "I'm just askin' you if you know where Ted is."

"You and about twenty other guys," was his reply.

"What's that supposed to mean?"

"Fuck you."

He pushed with all his might. I dug in, pushed back, and made my way in, shutting the door behind me. I kicked over the video screen and yanked out the gun.

"From what I've heard, you're a lousy comic," I told the guy. "Sit down."

The gun didn't make the fucker docile. His narrow eyes widened and took on a possessed, crazy look. He spread his feet, bent his knees a bit, and faced me like it was fourth and one and we were opposing linemen coming up to the line of scrimmage.

"You don't scare me!" he screamed over a punchline to a dumb joke we were missing.

I pulled the plug on his tape machine, stepping on a small slice of pizza as I did so. Dirty plates were on the tables and floor, paper bags and take-out food cartons were strewn about. The place smelled like a sewer, but contained an easy five-to ten-thousand dollars-worth of electronic gadgetry. The only light on now was in the kitchen, but I could see well enough as he dodged sideways, stooped quickly, and came up with a small nickel-plated dumbbell which he threw at my face. I ducked in plenty of time.

I came up to him and pointed the gun at the center of his forehead.

"You don't have the guts to use it!" he screamed. "Go ahead, you fucker. Go ahead!"

"You really want me to, don't you?"

"Yeah, yeah. I want it, sure, you fucker!"

I knew I was going to have to fire the gun to calm him down. This situation had something to do with the possibility that somebody else had gotten to him first, somebody he hadn't liked, who had made him wary of any others who might be seeking information about Ted Aikens. That was a distinct possibility. It was just as likely that he might have behaved in the same manner if you'd asked him what time it was or tried to solicit a paper subscription from him.

I didn't know. I wasn't sure. I tilted my sights just above his head and fired a shot into the top of the wall behind his vinyl leatherette couch. It didn't work. The gun boomed like a cannon in the confined space, plaster shattered and cascaded before our feet, but this guy was absolutely out of his mind. He charged me like a fucking kamikaze. I set the safety, wrapped my hand around the revolver, hooked, and caught him flush upon the jaw. He skidded forward, went down on his face, and lay silent.

Somebody was yelling outside. I pocketed the gun and moved toward the door as Broderick barged in wearing a knee-length orange kimono that glowed in the dark.

"I told them all to stay put," he panted in deep, fluttery tones. "Keep their doors closed." He stared down at the unconscious comic. "Did you shoot each other?"

"No."

"But a shot went off?"

"Yeah, right. How do I get out of here?"

"Men are so cruel," he opined, ignoring me.

"So are women."

"No. He's gone out of his way to make snide remarks to me. Well, I'm glad."

The set-up clicked in my head. I grabbed the old queen by his silky lapels. "He doesn't know where Aikens is. This is personal, isn't it? You wanted me to rough him up."

"Please let go," he demanded in his man's voice.

I tightened my grip and shoved him up against the wall. "What am I supposed to do now?" I screamed at him.

"You weren't his roommate," he pouted. "Everybody wants Ted Aikens. Could you tell me why?"

"Where is he?"

"You were friendly when you knocked on my door," he almost cried, his deep voice running with syrup again.

I looked at him. My face was up against his and I caught the full load of plaintive misery and pain knotted up behind his misted cow eyes. "Listen, I got nothing against you," I told him levelly. "Like they say, you're a woman in a man's body or something. It's not easy. Just tell me where Aikens is."

He started crying. "I love you," he said, his thick mouth blubbering with saliva.

I could sense people waiting outside the door. I let go of him and stood back. Broderick's kimono was bulging around the crotch. "You got this all wrong, my friend," I tried to explain.

"You're nice to me," he pleaded.

Somebody knocked on the door.

He had me at my wit's end. "Where is Aikens, please!" I practically sobbed.

He told me. I hustled toward the back door in the kitchen.

"Will we be in touch? Just for friendship—we could play chess," he called after me.

I hustled out into the alley, cut through a narrow walkway running alongside an apartment building facing the next block, crossed the street to the tune of approaching sirens, waded through puddles that threatened to sink me, and finally huddled down in front of a warm engine in an open car port that had an early curfew feel about it. There were three cars, a Rambler and two Fords, they were old models, immaculate. I hoped they belonged to senior citizens as I sat still and waited for bad news for over an hour. I had a hunch that Broderick wouldn't give away anything. I was glad I hadn't insulted him.

Eventually, I crawled out, shook out my wet legs and exercised them down to Santa Monica Boulevard, turning up Wilcox and walking brusquely until I reached the car. I wouldn't have been surprised if a whole platoon of riot-readied National Guardsmen had jumped out of the neighboring bushes and surrounded me, but they didn't, so I got in and drove away.

20

I wanted to go ahead and check out the address Broderick had given me, but I was afraid to push my luck again that evening and knew I should wait until the next morning when I'd have a little better chance of not running into somebody's stakeout. I was starting to buck bad odds, though. Too much was going on. I thought of calling my cop friend, Steifer, telling him what I had, and throwing the whole mess in his lap. I knew he'd do his best to help me, but he wasn't an independent operator, and what if somebody else behind him screwed up? You can't trust the cops to do the job right, not when your kid's life is at stake. I couldn't go about it that way, but all I had was one lead that I wasn't sure about. If that fell through, I'd be right back where I'd started. My clothes were soaked, I was bone cold, shivering, but sweating, my breath kept fogging up the windshield and I couldn't figure out how the heater or defroster worked. I got out of my absurd Columbo coat and flung it behind the seat, then I pulled over, took off my shirt, and put on the leather jacket. I mopped my face with the shirt. The coolness felt good over my fever.

When I got home, the roof was leaking in the kitchen. I put a frying pan and a Pyrex bowl down on the floor, then went into my bedroom, took the *Times* out of its sealed plastic rain wrapper and pretended to read. Alfie Wilde's obit was in the right hand corner at the bottom of the first page. The photograph portrait was from his youth. His thick wavy dark hair was parted in the middle and plastered down over his low forehead. His mouth leered uncompromising ambition. He was ready to rape, pillage, and sack all he could get from the infant film industry. It was a look that would work its alchemy in transubstantiating art from money, money from art. It wanted everything that had anything to do with passion. He hadn't looked that way when I'd met him.

I tossed the paper on the floor, sat, and thought about Sam and how she was probably pissed that I hadn't called or showed up at Burbank that afternoon. She probably wanted her car back. I didn't care. I'd been up and down every rung of the ladder in my house, but it had never felt so deadly quiet as it did now. I drifted through the bathroom and kitchen into Petey's bedroom in the livingroom. Everything was there except for Petey and Stanley. Seconds were popping off on his illuminated digital clock radio. His rollerskates and skateboard were underneath his day bed. Bruce Lee kung-fu posters and assorted playbills from rock concerts and local punk clubs decorated the walls around it. A team autographed Dodger baseball, numerous underground small-label 45's and LP's littered the top of his dresser. He had flash pins—the kind that shift images, palm trees to naked hula girls, skulls to crossbones—and buttons: *DISCO SUCKS*, FUCK YOU, and "FEAR," "X," and the "GERMS," his favorite groups. A birthday card from last June with the silly limerick I'd written him; a Polaroid of the three of us sitting on a picnic blanket at Griffith Park, with Petey and me in our matching leather jackets.

I pulled the spread up, made the bed, then went back into the kitchen, thinking about the old girlfriend who had taken our picture at the park. Ellen. I had lived with her, the three of us had lived with her. I couldn't remember why it hadn't worked out. Something complicated on her part. She was fresh out of college and hadn't been sure about her role in terms of responsibility. We had decided it was best for us to see other people. Soon, after passing through a maze of many stops and starts, we had both ended up with someone else. And the cycle had started all over again with a new partner. Maybe that was how it was supposed to be. The married people I knew, those who stayed married, didn't seem so happy. Maybe permanent relationships, all kinds, had become obsolete in terms of social value . . . . Maybe we were a dying breed at the end of its physical and spiritual tether . . . .

Hard to say. I certainly wasn't getting anywhere thinking about it, and my leaky roof was getting on my nerves. It punctuated the dead quiet, made it worse. There was no way I was going to spend the night in my house. I got out of the wet clothes, took a hot shower that did me some good, put on some thick cords, a sweatshirt, and a pair of boots. Then I went back down the hill, stopped at Greenblatt's for a half-pint of Cutty, continued west to Ben Frank's Coffee Shop, parked my tired ass in a booth, and ordered a pot of tea. When it came, I laced it with Cutty, sat back, and sipped my hot toddy. The effect was medicinal. It warmed me, cleared my sinuses, charmed my nerves, and put the lids back on my snake baskets.

I started thinking about Susan Grady and, before I knew it, I was standing in front of her door again. She wasn't going to get rid of me that easily. The scene was the same. The cars were parked in all of the same places. The rain was coming down and shining over the shattered white hexagonal tiles in the walk. A small, vaporous cloud wisped upward and disappeared into the dark above the streetlamp. No light in her apartment. I hoped it was early instead of late. Last night she'd pulled up around three, now it was fifteen after two.

I went back to the car, drove up a block and parked on a side street. I put on the jazz station and sat there drumming on the wheel, trying to keep time with a Miles Davis trumpet solo. Miles didn't need me. I didn't need Miles, not in this mood. I nixed the radio, got out, and walked down to Susan Grady's. I stood in my spot just beyond the northside row of cut-down rose stumps to the side of the downstairs lower left front window. There was a tall hedge behind my back. I stayed close to it and got a little shelter from the rain.

The limousine glided up about twenty minutes later. The pudgy uniformed chauffeur brought her up the walk underneath the wide umbrella and left her at her door. I waited for all the right sounds, saw the limo's headlights move away, and stepped out of the shadows. By the time I knocked, she was halfway up the stairs again. It was silent. I heard her coming back down, then stop. I knocked to assure her she wasn't hearing things, again. She continued coming down.

"Yes," came her tentative voice.

"It's me again," I said.

"Go away."

"I need you."

"Go away."

"No."

Silence, then: "Please go away."

"I can't."

"Why can't you?"

"Because I want to talk to you about last night. I want to know about you and your relationship to block-long black limos."

"I find them sexy."

"I see."

She opened the door. "Do you?"

There were lines for that. Right then, I couldn't think of them. She was gussied up again, this time with a broad-shouldered blue gray overcoat open over a high-necked, scroll embroidered jacket with a long velvet skirt and high boots. The embroidery was silver, all the rest black. It made her face too pale under her feathered Tyrolean hat. She pulled on a short cigarette, then flicked it to the side of me where it extinguished itself in one quick sizzle. As the smoke cleared, I started smelling gardenias.

"You wanna fuck me again, don't you?" she said simply.

"Yeah."

"Because we're both trying to forget something we'd rather not talk about. Isn't that right?"

I nodded once before I took her in my arms. She laughed as I carried her up the stairs.

"You don't care that you're giving me your cold," she said at one point as we were kissing.

I stopped. My jaw hung open. I didn't know what to say.

"It didn't even occur to you."

"No," I admitted.

"That's what I mean," she said by way of explanation.

Abruptly, she sought my lips and fastened on me before I knew what I was going to say or do. Then she fell backwards in my arms, pulling me off-balance. She had her teeth in my lips. Not that I didn't want to, but I had to go with her. We toppled to the floor just inside her apartment.

We made love again with our clothes on. In the dark.

21

The rain had stopped by the next morning. I woke up at eight-thirty with the sun in my eyes. I'd spent the night on the livingroom couch with an afghan over me and the pillow beneath my head had a pearl satin cover that smelled of gardenias. I studied it closely. There were red hairs on it that glittered in the hard fresh sunlight. Before I sat up or called out for her, I knew she was gone. I called out anyway, then I went into the bathroom, got out of my cords and sweatshirt, and took a shower. I couldn't remember much about the last night. She had gotten up afterward and left the room. I'd moved over to the couch and stretched out, waiting for her to return. Then I'd fallen asleep.

My nose had stopped running, but I had a bad sore throat now. I shaved with her leg razor, then I went into the kitchen and tried to find some tea. My leather jacket was slung over one of the director's chairs at the table. Some notepaper was scotchtaped over the flap of one of the pockets, from which the butt of my gun protruded. It said: "Interesting!" and pointed toward the gun butt with an arrow. There was another note on the table. "Hot coffee in the thermos, wheat bread, fresh eggs in the frig." Just commas, no period, and unsigned. There was a place setting for me with cup and saucer and matching plate in a dark blue ceramic. It looked nice on the white table, but she wasn't there. I was mad at her for not giving me an explanation, but then neither of us had shown a particular aptitude in that department. I had three cups of black coffee, then I put on my jacket and left. I didn't leave her a note.

The air outside smelled like freshly mowed grass. The smog had gone into hiding and the sky had been washed a bright limpid blue. The huge starched white clouds hurt as they rolled across my eyes. When I got up to the car, I felt like the last two nights hadn't really happened. I'd never seen Susan Grady under anything stronger than porchlight. Her image, to me, was flitting and wraithlike. It hadn't burned or etched its way into memory. We'd hardly talked, we'd made love hardly touching. Though remote, the stark, shifting clouds were far more tangible. Susan Grady was a schoolboy's wet dream, unsettling, difficult to remember.

I was low. We'd hidden from ourselves, taken refuge, and now I was back at the starting line. I hated Susan. Why hadn't she helped me? Why hadn't I helped her? We were afraid of each other, cowards. We neither knew how to take nor give. We had bought time and that was why our farewells were nameless. We didn't exist.

Right now, at this moment, my son was somewhere alive or dead. I had to find him.

22 ....

I got angry when somebody tried to waste my time. He came out of nowhere and tapped me on my left shoulder. I was in a gas station on Santa Monica Boulevard, filling up the Ferrari.

"Unique," he said. "A Ferrari owner pumping his own gasoline."

"Force of habit."

"Very nice car."

"Actually, it's not mine."

"Oh?"

"Belongs to a friend."

He was an older guy in fairly good shape, five-nine, five-ten, on the thin side, with a full head of wiry gray-black hair, wizened pockets about busy brown eyes, and a short meticulously trimmed white beard. His face and hands were deeply tanned. The rest of him was covered up by a plain gray sweatsuit and high-topped white leather tennis shoes that seemed a little simple for the three or four heavy gold chains around his neck and the clunky Rolex on his small wrist. There was something smug about him, but I couldn't put a finger on it. Maybe he was the first man to conquer sweat; there wasn't a drop on him or the hand towel he wore for a scarf. Or perhaps it was the way he said nothing with such glib, deep-throated confidence; after all, to my thinking, his bullshit hardly rated a tap on the shoulder.

He didn't look over when the sedan on the other side of the pump started its engine and drove away. I had thought it was his car. Quickly, I began to think I should wonder, but then my eye caught hold of a large object sitting by the curb that made his presence slightly clearer to me.

I hung the nozzle back on the pump.

"What do you want?"

His busy eyes narrowed and the wrinkles moved around them as his face gave me a big show that it was amused. He tugged on the ends of his towel.

"Just to talk."

"Give it to me in shorthand. I'm in a hurry."

"We have a mutual—how shall I say?—friend, Susan Grady."

"I know. I recognized your car."

"From where?"

"I saw it leaving Susan's the other night."

"You keep late hours, don't you?"

"Yeah. Is it any of your business?"

"No, of course not. You had no way of knowing."

"What?"

"That Susan and I are engaged to be married."

I scratched my head. "No. I don't believe she told me."

"Of course not. Why would she? She was upset. We'd had an argument. I'm Marv Fisk. Glad to meet you."

He put out his hand. When I didn't take him up on the offer, he just smiled sympathetically like he'd been doing and nodded a little to demonstrate how he understood.

I walked off to pay the attendant. The man was still by my car, standing up against the driver's door, when I came back.

"This could end up being too catty," I told him.

He put his hand on my arm. "That's not what I'm after. Believe me."

"I have to go now."

"Just tell me, vou met Susan very recently, didn't you?"

"Uh-huh."

"Just tell me, this is embarrassing, but she didn't say anything about me, did she?"

"Uh-uh."

"I wouldn't want anybody to get bizarre ideas."

"Like what?"

He lowered his voice melodramatically, mocking a stagey narrator: "A double agent provocateur, a man with a secret terrorist mission."

"Huh?"

"Susan's under doctor's care," he said, going back to the put-on of his normal voice.

"She seemed alright to me."

"Well, what can I say? I'm telling you the truth. When she's upset sometimes, she'll have an episode and, being such a fine actress, she's very convincing. You see, her parents died recently."

"So that's why you had to talk to me, just in case she said something."

"Believe me, once or twice it's been a problem."

"I just got out of your fiancée's bed and all you wanna know is whether she said anything about you."

"It's no one's fault but mine. She's a lady, we're both gentlemen. I blame myself, really. Susan and I had a terrible misunderstanding which, fortunately, to my relief, is all over."

"Uh-huh."

"That's the hard part, I'm afraid. She likes you, she really thinks you're a nice person, but, well, I've explained the situation. Susan was going to tell you herself, but I think this way is easier for everybody. She really feels bad about it."

"Oh, yeah. Well, I'll talk to her myself."

"I shouldn't tell you, but she's in the car. I know what it's like when everything's left up in the air. Maybe, for both of you, it's best to face it."

I walked over to the limo and looked in the back window. Fisk came up right behind me. Susan was slouched down in the seat. She had on a plain gray sweatsuit like Fisk's. Her hair was wild; her face was shadowed. She'd been crying. She was wiping one of her eyes with her sleeve.

The window went down. The chauffeur I'd seen in the rain was sitting sideways in the front seat with his face behind the morning paper.

"Hi. Is this guy pulling my leg?"

"No. Sorry."

"He says you're engaged. The two of you had a fight and you spited him by our fooling around."

She straightened up. "I didn't mean to use you, really. I was so confused. Please understand."

"But you sure fucked like you meant it, didn't you, honey? That second time on the floor last night, I'll be damned if that wasn't one fine piece of method acting."

"I wasn't acting. I was involved."

Fisk butted in: "At the time. But now it's over, huh, darling?"

"Yes. Please, let us go now."

"I'm not stopping you. Go ahead. Have a good life." Susan's loverboy put his card in my hand. "I hear you're a writer," he said. "Call me. We'll have lunch. I know people in the studios."

I dropped the card. The gutter was running high this morning from all the rain. The card fluttered downwards and fell right in.

"Win some, lose some. No need for sour grapes," he informed me as if he were trying to instil a sense of optimism in me.

I turned toward him and came up close. "You've done enough to impress her with your gallantry, fuckhead."

"Sir," said the pudgy little fellow from behind his paper.

"No," the man told him, as the side of his face twitched like it wanted him to do something.

Like drawing first blood, that inspired me to keep trying his patience. "I don't know why, but it's obvious she's scared shitless of you."

He backed off and composed himself. "That's where you're wrong," he smiled. "Susan is totally free. She can go and do exactly what she wants. We saw you as we were driving by and she asked me to tell you."

I bent down and looked back into the car at Susan. "Well, then fuck you both," I said, looking from her to him.

Loverboy stepped around me to get into the back of the car.

"You should do something about your vocabulary," he said nicely.

I was angry, sure, and I had more fight in me than I knew what to do with, but I was also so thoroughly humiliated, I wouldn't have touched the guy with a ten foot pole unless he hit me first.

It was killing me. I made one last try to get a rise out of him.

"Best *fuck* I ever had, sincerely."

He got in the car and looked out at me through the open window, smiling away.

23

Aikens was consistent. His new place in the Fairfax district, though a few miles farther west, was just as boxy and ugly as the last. His name was on the mailboxes by the garage, so I went up to his apartment on the second floor and knocked to no avail. I picked the lock with my Swiss army knife and Mastercharge card and went inside. The place had fresh paint, wall to wall brown carpeting, a low fold-out couch, boxspring and mattress without frame, and a beautiful quarter-cut antique oak roll top desk in the second bedroom. Empty boxes and suitcases were strewn about, most of them upside down with their contents dumped nearby. Every drawer was pulled and most of them were empty. There were broken glass jars upon the tiled kitchen counter, pots and pans upon the kitchen floor. Cigarette butts had been toed out on both the linoleum and carpet. I sifted through the pile of clothes and sheets in the bedroom, disturbed the already disturbed mattress and boxspring, then went for the desk in the study, stepping through a ground-cover of boxes and books that was an easy two feet high. A Smith-Corona manual, the same model as my own, sat on a pad on the center of the desk. Typing paper, a step outline for a feature length project entitled "Driving School," news items clipped from the daily papers, notes about plot and character that seemed related to the outline were interwoven with the general debris. The books were mostly hardcovers. Some of them, I was sure, were worth something as collector's items. He had a subscription to *The Hollywood Reporter, Variety,* and *Casting News.* His eight-by-ten glossies peeped out at me from beneath a full set of Mark Twain. I kicked the books aside to get at the pictures.

It was a casual profile of a rugged, square-chinned face chewing thoughtfully on the earpiece of a pair of sunglasses. The eyes were a bit squinty. There was a thick moustache and short, unparted, fluffy hair for decoration. I couldn't figure out if he was soft or tough or somewhere in between. Maybe he couldn't either. His name and G. *Brenner & Associates* and a phone number graced the lower right-hand corner in slanted script. I called the place and pretended I was inquiring about representation, finding out that their specialty was extra work. As I hung up, I thought I had the scenario of a struggling writer who paid his bills by hanging out on shoots two or three times a week. I had written porno. This guy was an extra.

I was betting on getting ahold of a datebook or maybe some more phone numbers, but I couldn't find a thing. My hunch was that Aikens hadn't been here for days. He knew how hot he was. Finally, there was one thing, a brochure with a recent postmark from a place called *Total Sun*. It was a tanning clinic, one of the new fads. There was a list of reasons pertaining to why you should try it. It was safer than regular sunshine, took only two minutes a day for a total tan, and was cool to boot. You had to join if you wanted to "keep that healthy, wealthy, and just-vacationed look of yours year-round." The whole thing smacked of the Doonesbury comic strip, but Aikens apparently took it seriously. He had called and gotten the price schedule for daily, monthly, and year-long membership.

This was a pathetic lead, if you could call it that, but I had nothing else to go on, so I pocketed a few of the glossies and drove up to Santa Monica and Doheny. *Total Sun* was on the second floor of a new office complex faced off with red brick, stainless steel, and dark glass. It was time to dust off my Detective Gillis persona and try my luck with him again. I had a great idea, far superior to wingtips and a trenchcoat or flashing my library card for ID. I parked up the block and walked back. When I got to the exterior staircase, I shifted into high gear, taking the stairs two at a time, then I sprinted down the outside passage, flung back the entrance door, and rushed in, brandishing the gun.

Facing me from behind a wide counter of varnished light ash, a slight young fellow with deep blue eyes, a close brown beard, and a burr head of dyed blond hair, had been sipping with a straw from a small carton of orange juice. The carton fell out of his hand and spilled over onto the counter and Pirelli floor as he jumped off his stool and stepped back against the slate-colored wall behind him. His hands went up above his head.

I pointed the gun at him. "Is he here?" I demanded.

"No," he pleaded, after a deep swallow for his breath. "We just opened."

I lowered the pistol and pretended to breathe a sigh of

relief. "Good," I smiled. I took the pictures out of my pocket and showed one to him. "Do you know him—is he familiar to you?" I rattled off authoritatively.

"Yes," he nodded hesitantly.

"Yes, you know him or yes, he's familiar."

"He was in yesterday morning."

"Is he a member?"

"No, I don't think so. He paid for a daily pass."

"This is an extremely dangerous man. Look at him again. You're sure he doesn't just look like somebody?"

He shook his head. "No, it's him."

An emaciated girl with punk-styled black gold tabby hair came toward me from the back of the side hall. Her eyes were wide, dark, and slow. She was open-mouthed and her bottom lip looked weighted down. Her black vinyl jumpsuit hung loosely over her boniness. I let her see the gun and motioned for her to join us.

"Yeah?" she said coolly.

"Listen up," I began, eyeing her with some cool disdain of my own. "Look at this." I handed her the other picture. "This guy's a mass murderer. He's gonna be here before noon or a little after. We've been on him for over two years, and—"

"You a cop?" she said.

"How do you know he's gonna be here?" he said at the same time.

"Cop, yeah. I can't tell you anything. I got a half-dozen plainclothesmen expected here within the half-hour. What I want you kids to do is pick up your personal belongings and clear out for the rest of the day. Take the petty cash."

"But—" the blond boy started in.

"If you have any questions, call West Hollywood and ask for Captain Steifer. If he's in, he'll try to answer your questions. Now, hurry. I don't want you gettin' hurt."

I walked over to the door, opened it, and pretended to

nod to somebody outside. That did it. I had those kids out the back door in less than two minutes. I even gave the blond boy a quarter for another orange juice and took down the name and number of the owner so I could have somebody call and explain what was going on. Then I mopped up the spill around the counter and walked around to familiarize myself with the set-up.

There were ten tanning booths, side by side, each with a windowless wood door that matched the grain of the front counter. Inside, all the booths were about four feet square. As you opened the door, you faced a panel of eight six-foot lamps that looked like fluorescent lighting fixtures set behind a thick shield of clear glass. The walls and doorbacks were covered with metallic reflectors.

The control panel, with separate timers for each room, was under the front counter. There was a large box of eye goggles for protection from the strong light on a shelf next to the control panel. When I flicked on the radio, speakers went on in all ten rooms. I turned on the ultraviolet lights in one of them and walked back and opened the door. The effect was blinding. I turned away, shut the door, and went back to the front desk and waited.

As I sat there, I had all the time in the world to think over my situation. The more I thought about it, the worse it got. Sooner or later, those punks would wise up and call the police, and I'd be waiting for them like a sacrificial lamb. But what did that matter? I wasn't worried about myself, I was worried about Petey. I'd do anything for that kid. Anything. He was my flesh and blood, more even than if I'd fathered him. He couldn't belong to me because he had started out belonging to no one. When you begin life getting kicked around like a can, later on, no matter what happens to change things, a part of you lags behind, keeping light and empty inside when it comes to forming attachments. You may be quick to trust, but you're just as fast at tearing things asunder. It's like you're that fucking can and if somebody kicks you while you're light and empty, it hurts a whole lot less than it would if you were full.

I knew it all. I understood. Petey was the mirror image of what I'd been like and knowing this should have made it simple for me to help make life a little easier for him. But I'd turned the kid against me. It wasn't just this time, it was cumulative. Sure, he'd been angry for no apparent reason and I'd been the target, but I'd acted just the way he'd wanted me to, hadn't I? I'd thought I owned him. Nobody owns anybody, least of all a kid like Petey. And I'd told him off like a stranger. You can talk to your kid like an adult, but when you tell him off you have to remember he's a child who hasn't fully developed his emotional muscles. You have to be careful. You have to at least try to control yourself. My old man had beat the shit out of me. What I'd done to Petey, the things I'd said to him, was just as bad.

"Sticks and stones can break my bones, but words can never hurt me." I said it aloud. "Bullshit." Language can kill by long distance. It can order nations to war or haunt the soul with corrosive memories that linger and wax stronger over time. Language is the meanest mother-fucker. I'd take sticks and stones any day—they kill one at a time without echoes.

And you can't forget they're gonna hit the road. It's just a matter of when; and you want to keep them long enough so that when they do, they'll survive. I'd failed at everything I'd wanted for the kid. I was a lousy example, what did I expect—that I could actually provide a decent home for a few years, help the kid understand himself, give a little happiness, get a little in return?

"No, no, of course not. Too simple," I told no one.

I was crying. "Motherfucking sonofabitch." I pounded the counter. I cried some more. I stared at my motherfucking gun, then I put it to my head. The blood was bamming through me, my arms and back were tight like I'd been pumping iron. I was crazy.

"You fuck-up!!" I yelled at myself. "Fuck-up!!!"

I had the snout against my head. My hand was shaking. The gun was prodding my skull. I yelled at myself a few more times, then I lowered it. I hadn't chickened out. I'd made up my mind—completely. I had to find the kid, find him good and alive. If I didn't, I'd made a pact with myself. I was going to blow my brains out. That's all there was to it.

24

If I'd been the sort of guy who got suicidal every time the Rams lost or his baby left him, I would have been a goner years ago. Sure, I can get maudlin, excessive, but this was the first time I'd ever thought of putting a gun to my head. Suicide was always somebody else's problem, a disease that happened to the other guy—that's how the game is rigged. But even loaded dice don't always drop the way we'd expect. If you're not too thick, after a while you learn that anything can happen to you. There doesn't always have to be a reason. Suddenly, the bottom can drop out, then, just as quickly, you get the funny feeling that all you're doing is filling up space, taking up some other guy's elbow room . . . and you decide to cash in your chips. That's right, Jack. Anything can happen to you. You better believe it. So, don't think you're too big. Don't be too proud. Remember.

Well, being a neophyte initiate to the existential ax act, I wasn't sure how the pros felt about it, but once I came out of my final reckoning powwow, I had that intoxicated, born again conviction so popular nowadays in politics. I felt jolted, supercharged with a sense of mission. It became much easier to think over and plan what I'd have to do. First, there was waiting for Aikens to show up. I figured it was unlikely, but I'd give it another two, two-and-a-half hours. Then I had to get my mitts on $100,000, and I knew how to do it. There was this guy I knew who used to work on my car, and there was this friend of his, so he'd bragged, who'd made a fortune on working over hot cars and shipping them to Mexico City. I decided to take him up on his macho bullshit chatter and called to ask what his friend could do with a hot new Ferrari. I was supposed to call him back in two hours. I figured whatever I didn't get up to the $100,000, I'd borrow on.

After that, the sunworshippers started trickling in. They showed me their membership cards or paid me four bucks and I set their timers and pointed them toward the sweatless ovens. There was a young lady wide as a house who must have been praying that a tan would make a difference. There were beanpole actresses and models who had professional reasons, a black man and a pale blond boy who must have had their own when they took the same booth for twenty-eight minutes longer than it took the clock to run out on their tans. I just manned the desk and handed out the eye goggles without asking questions.

The crowd thinned out around lunchtime. I looked outside, took a breath of fresh air, and came back in as a fair skinned strawberry blonde came bounding up the stairs, looking stern and business minded in a loose white turtleneck sweater over mauve colored jodphurs tucked into white cowboy boots. Her face was red and blotchy, her nose especially burned and peeled. She proceeded to berate me and the *Total Sun* salon for ruining her face and causing her severe stress and emotional torture. She was a model and we'd destroyed her for at least six months. She was organizing a class action lawsuit. I nodded along, said she was absolutely right, and offered to give her money back on a year membership. That took all the fight out of her and then she wanted to know what I thought she'd done wrong. I told her she'd gone a little too fast with the process, possibly. That made sense to her and she ended up opting for a thirty second treatment. I couldn't talk her out of it—something about getting rid of her dead skin and priming the new pigments.

After she was safely ensconced, the entrance door swung back and Aikens walked right in. It took every bit of self-restraint in my body to refrain from jumping him immediately. I had to get rid of the model first. He was on the short side, but stocky. I'd have to be careful. Blue jeans, black and white saddle shoes, a red shirt worn collar-out over a blue crewneck sweater. His contact lenses were what had given him the permanent squint. His stride was short and choppy; that, and his voice, when he spoke, gave evidence of social discomfort.

"Hi," he said like a college freshman.

I gave him the nod, smiled.

"Gotta get ready for some beach blanket bingo," he said, with embarrassment.

"Picture?"

"Yeah. Crowd filler."

I shook my head, commiserating. "And they still want you tan."

"That's the God's honest truth."

He got his wallet out and gave me a five-dollar bill. I

opened the register and tried to stall him until the model came out, but she was taking her time getting dressed. I gave him his buck back, then told him to push his button in the booth and I'd activate the timer for one minute, as he'd asked, when he was ready. He grinned an embarrassed grin, said thanks, and walked down the hall to the booth I'd assigned him at the end.

The guy obviously had something on his mind. It seemed to be important to him that I realize he wasn't doing this for pleasure or vanity. It was a job—as if I cared. It didn't matter to me if the guy was Tarzan or Jane. I had him where I wanted him.

The model came out and started apologizing for having been obnoxious. I had the feeling that she was the type who liked to get you to come on to her so she could go home to bother her husband with the day's news that men were still hot for her. This kind could never get too much attention. She was hard to get rid of. I tried to be cold, but that just spurred her on. I thought of being crude and telling her I wanted to fuck her, but that would have inspired even more oratory, possibly another class action suit. Luckily, the phone rang, a wrong number, but I pretended it was an important call and said, "Yes, yes, yes," till she got tired of waiting and waved goodbye.

I wrote "Out for Lunch" on a piece of paper, scotch-taped it to the inside of the door, and threw home the deadbolt. Aikens had pushed his button. My first instinct was to barricade the door and fry the bastard to death. I wanted to, but there was no sense in doing it; besides, you can't deal with monsters by being one yourself. You have to keep a cold spot inside of you; you can't let your hatred boil you away. I tried to think of myself as a six-foot block of ice.

I set the timer and went down the hall. I pulled the

gun and came up to the door. I stood there and counted to ten. I wanted Petey. I also wanted to turn this guy into a side of beef. Ice, dry ice. Slowly, I moved the door back. The fan was on; rock music was blaring. When I had it free of the catch, in one fluid movement, I yanked the door outward and came in at an angle.

Wearing briefs, Aikens was facing me with the goggles over his eyes. His back blocked most of the ultraviolet light so I wasn't blinded. I came up on him, kicked his balls for a field goal, then shoved the short barrel in his mouth as the goggles came free; he screamed out and fell forward from the knees, his square jaw agape, his squinty dark eyes popping wide and dull.

He passed out. The ultraviolet lights shut off with the timer and the booth went dark, the fan stopped. I shut the door and they came back on. I let Aikens crumble to the floor and kneeled over him, straddling his legs. I slapped his face a few times. When he groaned and opened his eyes, I grabbed him by his fluffy hair and banged his head against the plasterboard covered by reflector foil. I punched his face and pulled him to his feet, giving him a short hook to the belly as I did so. He had a hard stomach. He was in good shape, better shape than me. I had to keep hitting him without putting him out.

"You're gonna talk, Aikens," I told him. "Hear me?"

He nodded up and down.

"Good." I slugged him in the stomach again. "Now, the thing is, I haven't decided whether or not you're dead yet—got it?" I swiped his face with the butt of the gun. "You tell me where my boy is and help me make up my mind."

"I don't know," he blubbered through bloody lips.

I kneed him in the balls, shoved the gun in his mouth and held him up with it as his knees gave again. "Bad thing to hold yourself up with—it might go off," I said cheerfully, adding, "The more we talk, the less mad I get. When I'm not talking or you're not talking to me, I got time to think. I get all upset." I slugged him in the neck. "Why'd you kidnap my son? Think I'm a multimillionaire? Talk, Aikens, talk. Know which is mine? Mine's the live one with the dog. Not one of the stiffs— get me?"

"It wasn't my idea," he pleaded shakily. "He was just there."

His eyes were like large shiny buttons, staring at me without moving. The next time I hit him, he closed them and started sobbing. "I didn't want to," he cried. "I didn't."

"Where's your partner then?"

"I don't know."

My hands hurt. I was sick of hitting him. I grabbed him by his hair and banged his head another time. He went out. I let him down. After a moment, he sobbed loudly. "I'm gonna kill you," I told him.

He put his arms around my legs and hugged himself to me. "No, no."

"I kneed him away. "Where's your partner?"

"He took the boy. I wouldn't go with him."

"Where did he go?"

"I don't know!"

"What part of town?"

Aikens lolled his head around, trying to shake it.

"When was the last time you spoke to him?"

"Couple days ago."

"Where?"

"Left me at that warehouse, took the boy."

I believed him. I told him what we were going to do and waited for him to get his clothes on; then I walked him out to the Ferrari, holding the gun on him from underneath my jacket.

I noticed something odd. When I'd looked outside earlier, down below a guy had been pulling away from the curb in a silver Chevy. That car was there again and the same man was sitting in it. We had to walk by his car. I looked back as we passed and started around the corner. He was leaving again, his front wheels were turned toward the street, his head was turned in the same direction, glancing back at the oncoming traffic. The back of his head was shiny-black with silver highlights. He was wearing a tan windbreaker. I turned the corner, got Aikens in the car, and started driving toward Sam's house in Malibu. I didn't want to see her, but I knew she kept a gun in her house and I wanted somebody to hold Aikens till this was all over. If she wasn't home, I was going to tie him up and leave him there with a note.

"Try anything, sneeze, I'll blow you away right here," I told him.

He nodded up and down, then dropped his chin toward his chest, cupped his nuts, and moaned.

"Shut up," I said.

He got quiet, rocking his head like a religious zealot caught up in the fervor of a prayer chant. I turned the radio on and off, fidgeting with my gun hand. For the hell of it, I asked Aikens about his master plan. He just shrugged.

"What did you get out of this?" I asked him. "Material for your writing?"

"We thought there'd be money."

"Like Charlie Chaplin's family paid for Charlie."

Aikens shrugged.

"You should have stuck to bona fide celebrities. Oh well, you never know, huh, Aikens? But what'd you want the money for?"

"I'm a writer," Aikens mumbled.

"Yeah, didn't I just say that?"

"Somebody was interested in one of my screenplays, and . . . and . . ."

"Oh, Aikens, I cringe for your stupidity," I sighed. "You wanted to produce one of your own screenplays. That's so naive it makes me want to cry."

"But it wasn't going to hurt anybody."

I could have told him where he was wrong, but it wouldn't have been worth the effort. "Do you realize what it now costs to produce the average film?" I asked him.

"There were other investors," he brooded.

"Still, that's a lot of bodies, isn't it?"

He failed to appreciate my black humor. He lolled his head and squeezed his nuts.

The sky started playing tricks again, going from sunshine to shadows one minute to the next. I knew it would be raining again before it was dark. I turned from Santa Monica onto Wilshire, passing by a Beverly Hills fountain surmounted by a stoic green bronze Indian.

"What prompted you and your partner to move out of the realm of the dead into the land of the living," I pried further.

Aikens mumbled something unintelligible.

I clipped the side of his head with the gun butt. "What? Speak, Aikens, speak."

"We had problems," he said feebly.

"That's obvious. But what made you think you'd have any better luck with live bait?"

"I told you, I didn't," he grumbled. "He wanted to. We were in a jam."

"What are you getting at?"

"We were hot."

"I know that."

"Somebody tried to kill us."

"Connected with one of the bodies?"

Aikens nodded.

"Green, Levotsky, or Crane?"

"The other one."

"Which other one?"

It was confusing. The body was of a tall, conservative-looking guy in his mid-to-late thirties. It hadn't been tagged. Aikens' partner had called the Johnson Funeral Home and gotten a number. Contact had been established. The dead man's "executor" had coolly explained that the family was willing to do whatever was necessary. The $250,000 asking price had been swallowed like a sugarcoated pill. An exchange point had been set at a small ranchspread outside of San Fernando. There, Aikens and his partner had been ambushed as they stepped out of their car. The night had saved them as they took off on foot across some fields. Al, Aikens' partner, was convinced they were up against the mob. He was in a panic to get ahold of some quick money and flee the country. Aikens, on the other hand, had become immobilized by confusion. He knew everybody was after him, but he wasn't sure what to do about it. He'd fallen back on his regular routine of extra work and had been motel-hopping to keep the wolf from his door.

I turned left at Westwood Boulevard. Aikens got edgy. He knew I was taking him to the funeral home and he begged me not to, saying they'd kill him. I told him to clam up and looked in my rearview mirror for that silver Chevy. It was nowhere in sight. A block down, Aikens went for the door. I swerved to the curb and socked him on the back of his head. He went limp. I shoved him down low on the seat and drove on. Two blocks down, I pulled into the service entrance to the Johnson Funeral Home, locked the car, and walked in the back way.

25

I came into a tiled hall with a marbled linoleum floor. A stainless steel door on the left was labelled Surgery—Private across a red enamel plaque. I continued straight ahead and passed through another stainless steel door that led into a carpeted hall replete with somber paneling and superfluous ceiling beams. Well-spaced wrought iron candelabrums graced the arches and lit the way with twenty watt yellow bulbs in the shape of candle flames. I floundered through a dark labyrinth of three or four identical corridors until I found Bill Johnson's office and went in to face his receptionist. She'd gone Mandarin for Saturday with a high-necked, iridescent rayon thing machine stitched with little gold junks, buddhas, and pagodas across an aquamarine field. Her hair today was a mousy brown with a long flip. It looked like the court wig of an American forefather.

She looked up at me with the phone under her chin, said, "I'll call you back," and hung up. Then she picked a butt out of the ashtray and blew smoke out of the side of her mouth.

"I have to see Mister Johnson," I told her.

"Yeah?" she challenged.

"Yeah."

"I think I better call the police," she said, lifting the phone.

I ripped the cord out of the wall.

"The police came after your visit. They'd never heard of you."

I went to Johnson's office and opened the door. He wasn't in there.

"Hey," she called after me, "are you crazy?"

I came back to her, leaned over the desk and, in one swift motion, nabbed her cigarette from between her lips. I gave her a wild-eyed look. "Yeah, you got it," I told her. "I'm *ker-razzey*. I got this little voice in my head. It keeps telling me to shoot you full of embalming fluid. You ever heard a voice like that?"

I stubbed her cigarette into the desktop's polished veneer. It made her gasp. Then I pulled the gun and held it on her. "Now what about the stuff Johnson didn't tell me about?"

She put her hands on her lap and fluttered her false eyelashes like she was scared. "I'm sorry, you'll have to talk to Bill. He keeps all the records."

"You're good," I marvelled. "Incredible. You're laying odds that I won't blow you away. The gamble's worth it for you. With Pops gone, what's the diff anyway?"

Her lips parted ever so slightly. She smiled like she was dreaming.

I fired into the pillows of the couch against the leaded windows. The sound made a cushioned boom. She patted her hair, giving me the same look. I grabbed her by the neck and lifted her from the chair. She gasped and panted for breath. Her fleshy hips made the tight, shiny material ripple as they jiggled around.

"Cunt!" I screamed at her. "Where's Johnson?!"

She kept gasping and panting as I eased up on her. Her lips were downcast and sneering; her gray eyes blazed contempt. I clamped down on her throat again, squeezed it, and shook her around. She got blue in the face.

"He wouldn't know," she wheezed.

"Then who's that stiff and who wanted him?"

"I don't know."

I pulled her over the desk. She was in her stockinged feet. She smiled again, this time with a look to launch a thousand ships. Like that asshole comedian I'd run into, this violence was having an opposite effect. The comic had gone psychotic with self-righteousness, she was going overboard with an otherworldly, joyous passivity. I didn't know what to do with her. I slapped her around. She kept smiling at me. I pleaded with her, cajoled her, confessed that they'd taken my kid. She sneered a little, whimpered, but, all in all, moved on to greater heights with a bowed, beatific grin somewhere between deserving the Nobel Prize or an Emmy. She'd slipped up enough to give me the feeling she had something, but I knew I was never going to get it.

Not from her.

The room exploded twice. The leaded windows showered through the air. A panelled wall shattered into splinters. We dropped to the floor. When I turned her over, the old sexpot was smiling with the whites of her eyes. Blood was gushing out of the pulpy mass of her throat. She made gurgling noises.

I got up and moved over to the window. Another shot

sounded in the back, then a silver Chevy screeched by in the street, heading north. I shot for the tires, hit the left front with my second shot. The car veered right, skidded over the curb, and rammed the streetside pump in a self-service station. The passenger door swung out and a small man rolled from the car and jumped to his feet in one fluid motion. He dove for the sidewalk and disappeared behind a row of parked cars at the second a tongue of flame leaped twenty feet high from the end of the service island, exploding the glass cashier's booth and the wall high windows of an adjacent store.

I jumped back, holding my ears, then I hit the street, crossing over to the other side of the short wall of parked cars. The hit man was long gone. Along the block, all the small stores and offices had emptied out. People lined the street. Burglar alarms started up; whining sirens were coming from the distance. I went back to the parking lot behind the mortuary, unlocked the car, and started to get in. The driver's seat was covered with glass. I thought it was from the explosion until I looked over at Aikens. He didn't look himself—most of his head was blown away. I kneeled down, gagged on my guts, then went around the car, opened the passenger door, and rolled him out. The windows on both sides were blown away. The shot had passed straight through the passenger compartment.

I went back to the driver's side, whipped off my jacket, and swiped the glass off the seat. Then I jumped in and screamed out of there. I kept my mouth shut. My heart was up in my throat, bouncing around. It felt like a Mexican jumping bean looking for an opening out of my body.

26

I jumped onto the San Diego Freeway and took it out past Northridge to Devonshire, where I proceeded west, prowling for the 76 station and 7-11 store that were supposed to signpost my turn-off onto a narrow access road near San Fernando. It was pouring again all of a sudden, and the rain was whipping in through the open windows. I stopped at a shopping center and bought some plastic tarping and electrical tape to put up some makeshift screens. They fogged up right away. I got the defroster on, but it didn't work on them.

I was starting to think I'd gone too far when a Standard station and a 7-11 loomed up on the right. Close enough. I turned between the markers and switched on my high beams. I saw a sign for the Chatsworth Reservoir. There were tract homes, ranch houses, and small farms scattered about here, some hilly lots and open spaces. The weedy damp ground had been drying into an ochre color. The darkening sky and rain were working it back into a slushy gray mud. This area used to double for desert prairies in many of the old Hollywood westerns. When I was little, I'd watched so many lousy cowboy pictures on the late show and the weekend matinees, I almost had a feeling that I knew the place without having been there before. L.A. had always been that way with me. It was familiar, it belonged in my unconscious; it enthralled me, enticed with all the ambivalence of a dream. Good, bad, indifferent things happened here, but somehow you believed they worked out; and even if they didn't, you kept believing. This city makes you soft and soppy, turns you into mush. Like a star-struck girl with an autograph album, you run amuck thinking there's an answer to be found here—all because you've spent too much of your life sitting in the dark. And the big screen begat a small screen, and the small screen begat you, wandering about in gray slush that smears the earth and sky all one, leaving you alone, bereft, fearful, dumb, and unprepared for your battle against fate.

I saw a long, flat ranch house above me on the left. It was a dirty white, faced off with faded yellow shutters. Dull red and trimmed white around the edges, an over-sized shed sat behind it. Its doors were off. A pair of wagon wheels were rutted into the ground to the side of the muddy drive. In between them perched a rusted mailbox. There were no cars anywhere. I pulled over and parked.

I sloshed around, peering in all the windows, then jimmied the kitchen door and went in. The electricity was off; so was the water. No food and just a few utensils in the drawers and cupboards. A rag rug and thrift shop specials in the living room. The bedrooms and closets were empty.

A few minutes later, I came out of the back shed and

looked up toward an overgrown thicket, covering most of what appeared to be an incinerator. It was up beyond the shed and to the left. The rain was guttering down from there, making a muddy channel out of what had been a footpath. Beyond this top area was a ridge. I wanted to see what was up there. I started for the path.

I heard something behind me and spun around, going for the gun in my jacket. A blur of yellow hit me with a flying tackle, sending me flat out and skidding over mud and gravel, carrying a truck which rode along on top of me.

I looked up at a big, wide black face under a floppy gray porkpie hat. The eyes were behind horn-rimmed coke bottles, but the fleshy lips were cracking wise with a chummy sort of soul brother smile. I put a knee in his back and tried to wriggle out from under him. He grunted, lifted himself up a bit; a huge pale hand appeared from under his yellow rainslicker, and he flipped me over with a flick of the wrist. I went up in the air a little and came down right on my stomach, getting my wind knocked out.

"Hey, what's happenin'?"

I fought for my breath.

"What you lookin' for anyway?"

"Fuck you," I said.

"If you be lookin' for that rendez-vous, you in the wrong place."

"And that's why you were hangin' out here," I wheezed. "So you could tell me."

"Man, I wasn't hangin' out. I followed you!"

"So."

"So, you got the wrong spot. This ain't what you was lookin' for."

"How do you know?"

He didn't answer right off. Instead, he fished around

in his pocket. He came up with his wallet, flipped it open, and showed me a police shield and a plastic ID card: M. W. Mathews, Detective, Gardena Police Department.

"Mister Crandel, I'm a detective," he said with some of the grits and cornpone gone from his voice. "Ah know the particulars of your case. It happens to dovetail w'my investigations."

"Investigations of what?"

"It's complicated."

"If it's gonna take you awhile, would you mind getting off my back?"

He asked me if he could trust me, then he rolled me onto my back, got my gun, and stood up, offering a hand and pulling me to my feet. We went into the house to get out of the rain. He took off his slicker, I took off my jacket, and we sat down, me in a high-backed overstuffed chair, him on the couch. He had thick legs that stretched at his pant seams. His belly perched over the waistband. It made the bottom half of him look little and stumpy, like one of those French porcelain egg cups with feet. He laid my .38 beside him on the couch, used the back of his hand and played sandpaper sounds over the grizzle on the underside of his weak chin. Then he scrunched his flat nose and made a face as he shrugged in his coat.

"I hates the stink of wet wool," he said.

"So, you're tracking down the body heisters," I sighed.

He took off his jacket and laid it over the gun, shook his head. "Incidental," he said.

"What's that mean?"

He held up his hand. "Whoa. That's not what I'm here for. That cop friend of yours, Steifer, he's your main man."

"Steifer knows what I've been doing?"

"Let's put it this way: You a pied piper. You bringin' them termites out of the woodwork. We never intended to use you, but you been hard to catch up with . . . I knows what you up to. George told me 'bout that boy of yours. I *know* you want him back and we are gonna give you our best protection until this be over."

"I don't want your protection. If that guy finds out I've got you covering me—"

"As far as your own person'l safety, he the least a your problems."

"You better explain yourself."

"Back in L.A., didn't that make you wonder?"

"Wonder what?"

"Tha' little gray hair Mexican. You almost hand deliver you'self to you' own funeral. An' he is *not* Aikens' partner."

"Who is he then?"

"That's what we'd like to know."

"But you say he has nothing to do with Aikens."

"Aikens an' his man, they got your son—I mean Al Butera, and no Italian connection, he do. We found Aikens."

"I didn't do that."

Mathews raised his hand into a stop signal. "I saw it. We know where you at."

"I wish I did."

He leaned over and slapped my knee, making with a soul smile. "Give you'self a shot a patience, brother. Patience, my man, *patience*." He paused, spread his hands out, palms up. "Tha' invisible man you hear about —invisible, that's right—he *was* city councilman, my district: Freeman, Robert W. Freeman. He has this idea: our part of town's gettin' kind of low-life, ya understan', 'cause they had this crackdown over Hollywood-way and now the ladies of the evenin' has no place ta go in Hollywood. They branches out and oozes over our way—in Gardena."

"So?"

He put up the stop signal again. "I'm gettin' to it, brother, I'm gettin' to it. Now, Councilman Freeman's idea is that, as far as Hollywood's concerned, the damage already been done. It's run down, everybody in the country knows, at least thinks, Hollywood has *de*-generated into a den a iniquity an' depravity. So, his idea is to let sleepin' dogs lie 'stead of sendin' 'em into our part of town an' runnin' us down also. *He* proposes that the city pass this zone ordinance which would make Hollywood your official adult entertainment center—sort of a first step in legalizin' prostitution, but the important thing's it would keep the rest of the city clean . . . *clean* . . . An' you can imagine all the interested parties in that arrangement."

"At least three," I said off the top of my head.

"Yeah?"

"The prostitutes and their pimps would stand to get screwed eventually with the tightened controls; the city would make a bundle with taxes; and the Hollywood Chamber of Commerce would shit a brick. Every legit business, every square inch of ground that's residential, all of it would turn worthless overnight."

"They say it don't work so well in Boston, but Freeman thinks . . . thought we different. He got up this initiative to put it on the city ballot. This be goin' on for about a week. They start down in Gardena and they be startin' ta branch out, they be tryin' ta git all those thousands a signatures. Meanwhile, he disappears four days ago—a popular man. People like his way of approach, and his bein' killed woulda put a damper on's the initiative gettin' where it belongs, so his wife's told to keep the lid on and we be startin' ta investigate. Investigation's coordinated all hush-hush, without nary a fart nor whimper's been the Captain's motto."

We laughed. I asked him if he'd found the Councilman's body. They had—a half-mile up the road, turning in between the 76 station and 7-11 store. Aikens had talked turkey. He hadn't made a mistake or bullshitted me. I told my soul brother I wanted to go over there. He said I wouldn't find anything, but offered to be my escort if I insisted on going. I was coming to realize that we were going to be like Mutt and Jeff. There was no way I was going to get rid of the guy, at least until they cracked this thing.

I slumped down into the chair with a groan. "So who's behind it?" I asked him.

"We not completely sure, but jus' this afternoon I think I got me some important figurin' done." He gave his knee a slap and put on a shit-eating, Clem Kadittlehopper grin; then speaking like a slice of white bread, country-style, added, "Ah, shucks now. Us colored boys got some brains, don't we?"

"Good Richard Pryor," I complimented him.

"Why, thank you very much, sir. You see, I knew we'd become friends."

"About this hunch . . ."

He spread his palms out again, scowled to himself, and looked serious. "Well, I talked with Missus Freeman, talked with her real good. I looked into them Freemans and, well, he had him this—"

There was a flash, then a deafening boom. Mathews crashed backwards and blew open from the chest. I was splattered with his blood. I dropped out of the chair as the second shot went overhead, dynamiting plaster from the wall. I got to my knees, grabbed onto the chair, and flung it back. The room flashed, I dropped as the chair blew apart. My gun was on the floor by me. I lunged for it, another shot missed, plaster dropped on my head. I got the gun and fired toward the door. It was the dark little man in the tan windbreaker. His hand was up over his eyes. He was firing wildly in my direction. My second shot hit him just below his throat. He fired into the ceiling as he fell backwards, bringing down a brass lantern chandelier and a great deal more plaster. Then he was still.

Mathews was moaning as I rushed over to him. His legs were up on the couch, the rest of him was on the floor. There was a puddle of blood spreading out from his back. His hands were clamped over the bloody pulp of his chest, pressing inward. His thick eyeglasses were gone and his dark eyes were large and glassy. They didn't seem to be looking at me. He started trying to sit up.

"Quiet, quiet," I said, holding his head down.

His eyes shifted. He smiled up at me with his teeth gritted. He made grunting sounds from the back of his throat. A bloodsoaked hand came away from his chest and latched onto my arm. His lips moved around as he tried to say something.

"Quiet," I told him.

Over and over again, his heavy lips formed a 'B'. He'd open his mouth, gasp, stop, then make the 'B' again. The fourth or fifth time, blood gushed out as his mouth opened. He let go of my arm, looked at me, and smiled with his gritted teeth. His hand fished around by his leg, found a pocket, disappeared, then came out closed up into a fist. He smiled once more, then his teeth came ungritted, his chin dropped down and doubled over his throat, and he was dead.

I got out his wallet. He had a fifty, two ten's and all the right ID. There were credit cards and pictures of three or four foxy black girls, all with Afros. According to his driver's license, he was just a few weeks short of thirty. Lying there with a hand over his chest, if you saw through the blood, he looked like an overgrown black kid hamming it up with his interpretation of Napoleon. He'd probably done that sort of thing. I could almost see him being the class clown, not the obnoxious type, but the kind who goes through life charming everybody's pants off. What he didn't have in intelligence or looks, a guy like Mathews would make up for with charm. He'd seemed smart enough, though he never would have given O. J. Simpson any competition as an all-American looker. That wouldn't have stopped a guy like Mathews. His wallet pics were testimony to his industry. His sweethearts would be heartbroken, so would some of his cop cronies. So would I. He'd been a damn nice guy for the fifteen minutes I'd known him and I was sure he would have gone far. That's what folks would say about a guy like this. How far he would have gone.

I looked at the black man's face. It was grayish already and the fleshy lips were bowed into a little smile. He was a child again, definitely. He'd gone far, farther than he'd ever planned on.

I turned around and moved over to the hit man. My first impulse was to kick him. I kicked him, kicked the dead killer in the seat of his pants. It doesn't do a thing for you, kicking a dead man. I opened the front door and walked out into the muddy front yard and let the rain come down on me. The blood was soaked into the arm of my sweatshirt. I rolled my head around my neck, wondered whether I was really alive, then walked back into the house.

I kneeled down beside the hit man and turned him over onto his back. His eyes were closed. I put a thumb over one of his eyelids, got it up and studied the eyeball. It was mostly pupil, with a thin shiny line of dark green around the edges. He could have been Mexican, Indian,

Persian, a Sephardic Jew—it was impossible to tell. His nose was bumpy and fleshy but neat. There were whitened hairline scars around his eyes and around his mouth and chin. His shirt was a plain white Calvin Klein and the windbreaker had a Beverly Hills label. His shoes were expensive glove leather and his hands had been neatly manicured. Nothing but car keys in all of his pockets. I got him out of the jacket and ripped it up looking for something and getting nothing. Feeling the guy up told me he was all muscle, maybe an ex-lightweight or just an accomplished street fighter. Finally, I ripped his shirtsleeves and found some homemade tattoos, faded crosses and such, straight from the Barrio. There were tracks, too, old scars that had healed over. It was a story that didn't matter, at least to me. There was nothing I could get from it that could tell me who had sent him.

I walked over to Mathews and stared at him some more. His hand was still clenched into a fist. I bent over him and pulled apart the fingers. A penny fell out, his only change. I picked it up. It was a dime coated with oxidized blood. I stuck it in my pocket.

It wasn't until I grabbed my jacket and walked outside that I realized I'd never killed anybody before. I tried to think about that. It seemed like it should be important. Somehow, it wasn't.

27

I sold Sam's Ferrari a few hours later at my mechanic friend's little rat's nest of a garage on Washington Place in Culver City. Eddie, "Fast Eddie" as I heard him called, was a fortyish, aging, beanpole grease monkey with raccoon eyes, black hands, a turned up button nose, and gigantic Adam's apple that bobbled around as he spoke slow and steady with a high squeaky voice. He wore his Dodger cap catcher-style and said he was doing the deal for his hot car buddy by proxy, though, after haggling for ten minutes or so, it became apparent that my buddy and my buddy's buddy were probably one and the same.

Eddie handled me smooth, like he did this every day. He was a pretty swift dealer for a guy who looked retarded. It was a good front. You would have thought he was an honest slug wedded to his daily grimy toil. I almost laughed at him while he got me coming and going. Still, I couldn't complain. Losing $5,000 on the car's broken windows for the time and inconvenience it would take to find replacements, I got $50,000 and a battle scarred VW as a finder's fee, plus another $50,000 on good faith and a two to three year time table at 20% interest. I chugged away in the VW, shaking my head and carrying a gym bag stuffed with a thousand hundred dollar bills.

It was five o'clock. I went to Petey's favorite restaurant, this little Chinese joint on Pico Boulevard where one of the waiters was a black belt in four or five martial arts and gave Petey an impromptu lesson every time we came for dinner. They had just opened and our waiter wasn't there yet. Everybody else knew me, the owner and the two other waiters, but they just nodded and said hello, which was just as well. I knew I shouldn't have come in, but I was there, so I ordered our three dishes: beef with oyster sauce, sweet and sour pork, and chop suey. I skipped the appetizer. I wanted to get up and leave, but I couldn't. That would have jinxed it.

After the food came, the owner approached my table.

"Where your son?" he asked me.

"Oh, he might be coming," I said, forcing a smile.

He went and got another glass of water and a pair of paper wrapped chopsticks and set them down across from me on the other side of the booth.

"Be here soon. Don't worry," he smiled and nodded, sensing something the way people do.

"Sure, thanks," I told him.

Some people came in. He hurried toward the front. I sat there, staring at those chopsticks and the empty seat. Time passed. Someone came, poured my tea, and served the order around a bed of white rice. I ate quickly without looking up. When I was finished, the owner was setting tables and looking at me from the other side of the room. I was afraid he was going to come over and talk to me again. I nodded back at him and put on another smile, then I got the check and left my money on the table.

At the door, I looked back. The chopsticks were sitting there. So was the glass of water, empty teacups, the uncovered food. I'd left half of everything behind.

28

I bought a pint of J.D., took it home, and waited for the call. I had a couple of shots, but they didn't help much. I closed up the bottle and thought over what Mathews had told me about the city councilman. Suddenly, it rang a bell as I remembered that peculiar assemblage of old fogies and young do-gooders I'd encountered at the skin flick a few nights ago and how it had been Greek to me what they were doing there picketing with their pro-porno banners. Now, I understood their cause. They hadn't known that their leader had been bumped off. In a day or so, there would be a press release. I wondered what it would do to their organization—scare them off, tear asunder or atrophy their cohesive purposefulness, or perhaps, with a charismatic replacement to spearhead the effort, inspire them to greater heights of tenacious destiny to fulfill the public welfare. You could never know. The only thing certain was that somebody wanted to stop them before they were noticed or did any harm, before it was too late. But who and why? What would happen if Hollywood became L.A.'s licensed adult entertainment center? Who would suffer? Was the mob behind it? Would this interfere with somebody else's operation?

The possibilities were mind boggling. The most obvious thing was that Hollywood commerce and real estate would be crippled, small and big businessmen would be out on their ears. If the initiative got on the city ballot, if the voters then went for it, the city would be buried under an avalanche of recall petitions and damage suits filed by every storekeep and bungalow owner in Hollywood. It would never work, not in Hollywood. The area was somewhat rundown, but they were still strong enough to fight it. Besides, there was a lot of money going in there lately. Old buildings were getting face lifts, Mann's Chinese Theater had been expanded, the Holiday Inn was adding a new wing. So who had been moved to such extreme measures by a radical right-wing cure-all that was nothing more than a will-o'-the-wisp?

The answer to that one seemed to absorb the population of modern day Athens—it was very Greek. I had another shot as I wondered what it all had to do with me.

The phone rang. I turned on the answer machine's tape recorder and picked it up.

"Knew you'd be home," said the shrill-pitched fast voice.

The craziness of it shook me, gave me a chill.

"Hello, you there?"

"I'm here," I said.

"Rainbow Room, Santa Monica and Western, thirty

minutes. Put the money in a paper bag. When you go in, have a drink. Drink some 'a your drink, then go to the men's room. Behind the toilet there'll be a sign —pick it up and leave the bag in the same place. Then—"

"Let me speak to my boy."

"Put up and shut up."

"What does that mean?"

"You'll see him when we're finished."

"Where?"

"Listen to your instructions!" He waited for my silence. I gave it to him. He went on: "You come back out, you finish your drink, you split. Outside, he'll be sittin' on the bus stop. But judge the time—less than five minutes, I get him, you, anybody steps in the way. You got it now?"

"Just let me say hello to him."

He hung up. I dumped the money in a shopping bag and got on my way.

29

Housed two doors down from the corner in between an army-navy surplus emporium and a used appliance store, the Rainbow Room was a dimly lit, foul-smelling haven for tired rainbow hunters young and old, white, black, yellow, red, or brown, all of whom had gone somewhere *way* over in their mystic quest for the legendary pot of gold, land of Oz, or maybe just a regular paycheck that could compete with welfare or unemployment.

A narrow wood grained formica counter ran the length of the left wall. There were chrome stools with soft square black seats. Crowding the right side of the aisle was a miniature bumper pool table with shredded felt that held broken cues and overstuffed ashtrays and two quarter tables where the main scene was happening in slow motion. At one, a mean-looking muscular black dude in high-waisted plaid pants, scuffed white patent leather half-boots, and a V-necked undershirt was smoking two cigarettes hanging off the opposite ends and playing solo. At the other, a slight, gray-haired drunken Japanese fellow was in tournament with a chunky Mexican wearing a white orderly's uniform who miscued, sending the white ball under the table belonging to the black stud. It caused a commotion. The Japanese *kibitzers* were all old farts who laughed and jabbered excitedly, poking their friend and exhorting him to exploit his advantage. He parried them away garbling slow guttural curses. The Mexican, meanwhile, lay on the astroturf floor beneath the other table. One of his friends walked over and nudged him with a foot. The others shook their heads, tilted back on tiny metal folding chairs, and drank. The black dude ignored everything and kept travelling slowly around his table, stepping over the comatose Mexican's legs when he had to.

None of them looked at me or realized I was there, except for the bartender who could have been either a Samoan or an Indian. Whichever, he stood about five-five and weighed in on the heavy side of two hundred and fifty pounds. He had shoulder-length wavy black hair, fat bulbous cheeks, a chin mole with long bristly hairs, and wore wraparound sunglasses. There were informal brass knucks—flat-edged, oversized silver and gold rings—on most of his fingers.

"Can I help you?" he asked pleasantly.

I gave him my full attention and ordered a draft beer, paid for it, drank, watched the drunks stumble through their game, then turned and stared at the clock, checking it with my watch. Five minutes. A semicircle of primary colors was painted on the yellowed wall around the plain clockface. I remembered Alfie Wilde's obit. It dawned on me that this was the place where he had offed himself. His guilt had driven him back here to try to make the contact he had first shunned. Money had probably been lifted off his corpse, a fat roll of green-backs that nobody would ever hear about. The heister had to have a reason for using this place more than once.

I finished the beer, got another one. I was sweating blood. The entrance door opened, there were traffic and downpour noises and a short, drowned rat staggered in, swimming in his baggy pants, oversized loafers and sop-ping navy peacoat. He sat next to me and ordered a beer. The barkeep asked to see his money before he poured it. The rat scratched his matted gray hair, grumbled, and came up with some coin. Mathews would have hated the smell of him. It was the odor of wet wool, a combo plate of cat piss sprinkled generously over a hefty serving of chilled whale shit. I took another sip of beer, got up, and went for the men's room.

Once I was in there, I unzipped my jacket, took the bag out, found the sign behind the toilet, and put the sack in its place. I turned around, saw myself in the mirror above the washbasin, and jumped out of my skin. Me, only me. My hair was wild, my face was pale and tense. The eyes belonged to someone else, someone who really hated me. Once, when I was sixteen, I'd had it out with the big cheese of a rival gang. He was nineteen, had tattooed arms the size of my thighs, and attacked me in a blind alley with a zip gun and a bowie knife. There was him, there had been others; I'd been up against it many, many times, but I'd never been as frightened of anybody else as I found I now was of myself.

I mugged around for a sec, posing, trying to squeeze the poison out of my image. But I couldn't. I pulled my hand back to punch at the mirror, stopped, took the sign, and walked out. OUT OF ORDER—FUARA DE

SERVICIO in big block letters. Thumb tacks were taped to the back. I took them off and tacked it up. Then I came back to my barstool and drank the beer.

The sewer rat was standing over by the pool tables. When he turned around, I looked at the clock. Before I knew it, he was sitting next to me again. It was almost twenty-five till eight. I started to get up. Out of nowhere, he slapped his hand over mine, pinning my wrist to the bar top.

"Too soon," he said with a gruff, quiet voice.

I jerked my head toward him.

He lifted one side of a gray toupee. "George Steifer," he said. "Christ, can't you tell? I'm wearing all your clothes."

I looked toward the barkeep. He was standing down the bar, watching the tables. I glanced back at George. "What are you doing here?"

Steifer muttered something unintelligible to keep up his front. I had no trouble playing the part of somebody he was irritating. I leaned the other way so it wouldn't be obvious we were having a conversation. "I staked out your house," he said next. "After you left, I went in and played back your tape."

I looked straight ahead. "You cops are gonna blow it for me," I said quietly.

"I'm by myself."

"Bullshit."

"Believe what you want."

"Do me a favor and get out of here."

"No."

"Fuck, man, *please*."

"I got no kids and I just shut the door on an eighteen-year marriage."

"What does that mean?"

"I like yours and I'm gonna help you. There's a back

door. I'll go stand by it. You go out front like the plan. If the boy's there, come back and get me. If not, fire your gun and I'll hit the alley. There's a window over the men's room—on the roof. He's gotta be comin' down that way into the alley. All right?"

"OK."

"Then let's go."

I got up and went out. The rain blew into my face. A black Eldorado and a new bronze Honda station wagon shined under the streetlights on my side of the intersection. Their side windows were fogged. The downpour speeded up, shoving the wind out of its way, and hammered at the sidewalk and car roofs. The light turned green, the traffic moved. The bus stops on both corners stayed empty. I sprinted two blocks east to the next stop, fired the gun, and ran north, cutting into the alley. As I did, a small car jumped me with its brights and shot forward. I dove back onto the sidestreet and rolled across half the pavement till I landed in the overflowing gutter beneath a parked car. The car made a sharp turn, skidding out on the rear, then squealed north up the side street. There was another car just behind it. I got up and ran for it as it made the turn. A door swung open on the passenger side. It screeched to stop. I jumped in as it was moving.

30

We were on his ass. Steifer's BMW had him on the wet streets. He swung left, then took a quick right on Wilton Place. We barreled after him, heading north. At the intersection of Wilton and Fountain, we overtook him. Steifer tried to sideswipe him into the parked cars in the opposite lane; instead, his front end caught us by the tail and spun the BMW headlong into the right hand curb. He was two blocks ahead when he swung left onto Franklin. The BMW's front end was wobbling; we were losing time. He swung right on Van Ness. We got a taillight going left on Foothill and lost track of him somewhere along Hollyridge Drive.

Steifer stopped. We listened, heard high revs and squealing rubber, and backtracked down the hill. We heard the same thing again and went back up. We turned up private drives, cut the headlights into cul-de-sacs, till we didn't know where to go.

Steifer was thinking out loud. He'd say, "Maybe down here . . . we'll cut left . . . that sonofafuckingwhoremother . . . we're fucked . . . no, let's bear right."

I couldn't talk. I couldn't think. Steifer thought we should cover the area on foot. He pulled over and got out, I followed on automatic pilot.

Half the streetlights and porchlights were out. We were walking through a wall of rain. You could hardly see where you were going, and both of us were wet to the bone. Steifer yanked off his wig and threw it into some bushes in front of a house. Within a minute, his dry hair was plastered to his head.

"What are we doing?" Steifer asked me after we'd been dragging around for a half hour.

"I don't know," I told him.

We walked some more. I became bitter. My bitterness prompted a question: "Why were you in the alley before I fired my gun?"

"It would have been muffled by the rain, I never would have heard it," he said.

"In other words, you just said that to pacify me."

"If your boy was at that bus stop, nothing could have hurt him. If he wasn't, I thought we had to catch the man."

"What if he was there and the driver gave some other guy a signal when you came after him."

Steifer put a hand up on my shoulder. "Ben, listen to me. Your boy wasn't there."

I shrugged him off. "But how did you know that?!"

"You gave him the full ransom, didn't you?"

"So what?!"

"A day and a half is pretty good for raising a hundred thousand dollars. He's planning to take you for more. I knew he'd do that. He's desperate and he thinks he can get it. I've seen this before."

I turned around and started walking away. Steifer caught up and grabbed my arm. "I was tryin' to help you. I don't know what else I could have done."

"It was none of your business."

He hauled off on the left side of my jaw. It was a good shot. I hadn't seen it coming. I blanked for a split second, but kept my feet.

"OK," I said, nodding to him and rolling my head around.

We walked back toward the car together without talking. We were a couple of blocks away when I heard a dog howling.

"Listen," I said.

"It's just a dog," Steifer shrugged.

"The kid had the dog with him."

We stood there, listening. Steifer looked at me. He was excited and trying not to show it. "Let's find it," he said.

I wasn't sure it was Stanley. The rain was playing tricks with every sound. Our voices sounded hushed, then tinny; the cars rumbled like speedboats and the water they swished through sounded like broken glass. When a cat squealed, first it sounded like a chorus of shrieking, irate birds, then segued into the squall of a colic baby. Besides, it was so good that, taking Steifer's cue, I didn't want to get set up for a big disappointment.

Weaving in and out of short streets, we wound up in front of a long little house with a prayer shaped wedged roof. The howling was from outside in the back. It was lit up like a Christmas tree—every inside light was on— and the front door was wide open. Houses on either side were dark. One was porchlit.

I started for the front door.

Steifer stopped me. "No. We walk around, take a look."

"All right."

We crept up the short drive, slid across the short puddle of a front lawn on our knees and elbows, got up, and looked through the kitchen window. Nothing. We moved across the front again, lunging one at a time over the path before the open front door. An overgrown hedge covered most of the front window. We moved around to the other end of the side front.

The dining room was lit glaringly by a kitschy crystal chandelier in the shape of a crown strung with glass beads. It glared down upon a long dark table with no chairs. A man was sprawled across the table, face down.

"They're gone," Steifer whispered.

The dog's howling grew hoarse and sporadic. We went back to the front door, walked in, and went straight for the dining room.

The dead man's blue jeans were soaked from the knees down, including his high-top sneakers. His leather flight jacket had a furry collar. Steifer turned him over. Blood spread over the table.

Steifer nodded toward the man's midsection. "Ripped his guts out."

He was bare-chested. His whole upper torso was awash with his lifeblood. He was over six-feet tall, thin, long-limbed, and roughly handsome with a fine, sharp nose and sculpted cheek bones. A full mantle of uncombed, dirty blond ringlets curled about his head. The blush of exertion was still deep in his blood-spattered, pale complexion. His mouth had settled into an open, slack-jawed expression. I don't know why but he looked like an alienated rich boy impersonating a street tough. Maybe it was because his uncalloused, long-fingered hands seemed a touch too elegant or delicate.

Steifer leaned over the guy's face, pulled his head up by the hair, frowned at it, studied it from both profiles and let it go. It made a thunk as the back of the head struck the table. Hideously puppetlike, the jaw aperture widened, the lips spread a bit. He appeared to have taken pause after hesitating to speak.

"Allen Butera, Aikens' partner," Steifer pronounced, shaking his head. "Real estate broker. Must have run out of deals."

We searched every room. The livingroom had a couch and stereo. There was nothing in the rest of the house. In the kitchen, we dumped the trash bags onto the floor. Beer cans, carry-out pizza boxes, two empty half-gallon milk cartons. There was a jar of grape jelly and a loaf of Wonderbread in the refrigerator. A bottle of Dox Equis was frozen solid in the freezer.

The dog kept up its hoarse cry. I looked out the window. The exterior floodlights backlit the downpour, making it look staged. There was a long cement strip with the faded outline of a shuffleboard court, an overturned barbecue amidst overgrown trees, hedges, and patchy grass. I opened the side door and Stanley rushed in, practically knocking me down.

I sat on the floor and held him in my lap. He was shivering bad. Steifer took off his pea coat and rubbed him down.

I got to my feet. We left Stanley inside and checked out the backyard.

Nothing.

31

"He may be OK. We got no reason to believe otherwise," Steifer said for what seemed like the tenth time.

We were heading downhill toward Franklin. Stanley was shivering on my lap, smearing his wet nose against the passenger window. Every now and then he'd make a yelp and wag his tail. I was vexed. I couldn't help thinking that there had to be something else we could do.

"Crandel, I'm sorry I hit you, but I'd rather have you raving mad than despairing."

"I'm thinking," I nodded. "Where we going?"

"Hell if I know."

"Pull over."

Steifer pulled over and turned toward me. "Toss it around."

"When was Mathews on to me?"

"This afternoon when the Mex put a tail on you."

"Who'd he work for?"

"We don't know."

"But they wanted that Gardena councilman out of the picture."

"Yeah."

"I wonder why."

"So do we."

"I been thinking about Mathews."

"Yeah?"

"Did he phone in any special leads today?"

"Not that I know of."

"I'm just thinking . . . He said that he'd come up with a lead . . . just this afternoon. It had something to do with the Councilman's family . . . then he got shot. He was trying to say something that started with a 'B', but he couldn't say it. Then he reached into his pocket. His hand came out in a fist, he smiled and died."

"Yeah?"

"He had a dime in his hand. I had to pry it out."

Steifer shook his head. "I don't get it."

We sat there and said nothing. Then it came to me: "Let's go to a pay phone."

Steifer pulled into a gas station. "Now what?" he asked me.

"Call your people, Gardena too. Find out if the Councilman had a brother."

Steifer jumped out and got on the phone. In three or four minutes, the booth light went off as he came out and scooted back into the car. "Freeman's got a brother, all right. Big construction *maven*."

"Got his address?"

"Two-twenty-one Mapleton Drive."

"Let's go there."

"Wait a minute."

"What?"

Steifer nodded to himself. "I see," he said. " 'B' equals brother and dime's the finish."

"He was a black dude," I explained. "Said brother this, brother that. But he took his work seriously. He wasn't going to jive-ass dying."

Steifer backed up. "Was he talking about sibling rivalry?"

"The guy seemed witty, but how witty can you be with your body lying in a number of pieces?"

" 'Brother, can you spare a dime?' Who knows?"

"Let's go see if it makes any difference."

"Right."

32

Sunset was swimming. It looked a little like an abandoned battlefield or the Indy 500. Every hundred yards or so, tanks and chariots were stalled or piled up along the road. Hoods and trunks were up. Cops rolled by dropping flares and, keeping close to their mounts, drivers in raingear and upturned collars flagged them down or peered around the bends as they waited anxiously and skeptically for the tow trucks that would set them back on track. Inside Beverly Hills, the hilly S curves were flooding out in their valleys. On the approach, the water slick road seemed to be layered by shallow puddles; once you hit them, many of these became as deep as three to four feet. Luckily, the worse points were earmarked by those who had faltered before us. Cars floated in the trouble spots and there was room to get by until we got close to where we were going.

High concrete embankments packed back the hillside on both sides of Sunset where the road had been widened at the base of a curvy stretch by Charing Cross. There were lights on a private tennis court cantilevered high above the road. We were on an asphalt hill looking down upon a small lake. White Beverly Hills police cars were parked across its shore, blocking access. There were five or six large cars sunken in the dark murk, a couple with just their roofs showing. The people who belonged to them were walking around, trying to figure out what to do. Steam rose from the water around the engines. One, at the far edge, kept turning over. Its lights dimmed and went out as I watched; its ignition stopped grinding.

Steifer pulled over, reached into his glove box, and took out a map. Then he remembered without looking, reminding me that Beverly Hills had once been his home turf. We turned onto Carolwood by the Jayne Mansfield house, parked the car, and walked over many long, dark, soggy lawns until Steifer said we were in a small exclusive suburb called Holmby Hills. We cut across a few estates, heard pampered watch dogs bark and growl at us from inside their master's lair, and ended up on a fairway of the L.A. Country Club. Steifer had done this before. He sloshed ahead without hesitating, and a few minutes later we were standing under a streetlamp on Mapleton Drive.

Steifer jerked his head at a high, wrought iron gate. "That's Hugh's place."

"Hugh who?"

"The Hef—Playboy Mansion West."

We walked a little further. Steifer jerked his head again, this time at a small, waist-high box stencilled with illuminated numbers. "Freeman's brother's right next door."

"Comely."

"That's what *she* said."

"Lee?"

"Come Lee, Hef, George, Phil—what the hell, it was a big party."

We tried smiling at each other and walked up the narrow drive by the illuminated box. There was a sharp incline that you couldn't see over. At the top, it levelled out and, a few steps further on, we came up against a tall mossy wall lit every twenty feet or so with dull little carriage lamps. A speak-box was in the wall by the barred iron gate. Beyond was a long, round-pillared porte cochere with two trellised lanes going in and out. Huge double white doors fronted an imposing three-story Georgian brick Colonial topped off with a slanted grayish mansard roof that crowned the edifice like a monstrous flat-top haircut.

Steifer pushed the speak-box button. In a moment, a timid voice asked him what he wanted. Steifer identified himself and asked to see Mister Freeman. We were told to wait. We waited close to five minutes. Steifer pushed the button and said hello a few times.

"Hello," another voice said. The sound was tinny, but there was an unmistakable resonance of sheer, unmitigated confidence. I didn't know why, but it sounded familiar.

Steifer stated his business.

"I'm sorry," said the confident voice, "but I have no idea who you are or what you really want."

Steifer sneered at the box and leaned closer to it. "I just told you."

"Yes, but how can I be sure?"

"You keep us standing out in the rain another minute, and you'll be very sure, I assure you, sir."

"Am I getting arrested?" was asked in a completely jocular manner.

"Maybe. I don't know yet."

"On what grounds?"

"Open this goddamn gate."

"Do you have a warrant for my arrest?" he asked in arch tones.

"Let's put it this way: do you want me to go and get one?"

The box went dead.

"I don't know what you're doing," I said. "If he's got Petey, he's probably hidden him by now."

Steifer frowned, waving a hand at the house and grounds. "Is this kind of guy gonna get into kidnapping?"

"Then what are we doing here?"

"We're desperate. We want him to give us a lead."

"Just the same, I want the house checked out."

"Suit yourself," Steifer shrugged.

One of the double white doors opened as a mechanical latch clicked on the gate. I pushed on it and we walked in while a short, pudgy man pulled on his cap, popped open a large umbrella, and trudged toward us over the bricked yard. He looked familiar, but I wasn't sure. He met us halfway, nodded perfunctorily, and walked back to the door standing between us. It was a nice gesture, but it really didn't help much: and I decided, after all, he wasn't too familiar-looking either. To a guy who doesn't see them every day, short, pudgy chauffeurs don't seem to be a dime a dozen when, in reality, they probably are. Besides, he was too short.

At the door, we wiped our soaking feet on a welcome mat and followed the pudgy man into the house. The chandelier in the entry must have weighed a ton. It dazzled, throwing brilliant patterns over the polished marble floor. The chubby underling disappeared and the legs of another man appeared descending the stairs. They were longer legs, slimmer. Then the rest of the picture came into view. He looked like a regular enough guy, rather youthful for his age. He was wearing tight designer jeans with a crew-necked black velour. His tan hadn't faded, the hair was still wiry, the beard was almost as neat as it had been that morning, though it was fuzzy now with stubble around the edges. He looked as smug as ever. When he pulled his sleeves off his forearms, chain linked gold bracelets glittered on both wrists. No watch and nothing around his neck. His feet were quiet in leather slippers.

He made a display of playing with his sleeves again, then he opened his hands and spread them out.

"You see I have nothing to hide," he announced, making a larger production out of his mouth.

He lost the happy look momentarily as he recognized me, but it came right back. "What kind of charade is this?" smiled the man who had called himself Fisk. "She's not here."

I wanted to smack the fucker on sight. Steifer showed him his shield.

"Who?" Steifer asked.

"That's a nice badge for a fake. You know."

"He thinks I'm looking for his girlfriend," I tried to explain. "By what may or may not be a strange coincidence, I met him this morning. I had a brief thing with his fiancée. He told me to stay away."

Steifer didn't get it. "You met her before or after Petey's disappearance?"

"Before."

The man, whose real name was Gene Freeman, tilted his head back and made a show of laughing. "This is a cute playact, it really is, but I'm going to have to call the police."

"Go to it. I could use some help," Steifer told him as he nudged me away. "Let's go over the house," he told me.

"Have a seat," Steifer told Freeman from the stairs "I'll be wanting to talk to you."

"I have nothing to say to *you*."

"Sure you do. Think about it. "

"Pa-shah," scoffed Freeman.

I turned around and took a step down. Steifer got me by the arm. "Look at your hands," he said quietly.

I looked at them. They were balled up into fists.

"Don't be a hothead," Steifer whispered. "That's what *he* wants. Remember . . . we got a lot to do. Come on."

I went on up trying to wipe the bastard's smile from my mind. We combed the place quickly, upstairs and downstairs. Saying nothing, Freeman tailed us, then gave up and walked away. It was a swank set up that oozed expense and luxury, but it was wasteful and ultimately cheap, not all of it, just the rooms that didn't look like they were used—which was most of the place. The livingroom had everything: trendy abstracts, airbrushed butt, thigh, and panty fetishes, odd bits of glass and polished chrome, comfortable couches, and plenty of electronic gadgetry. It was camp trash that, at its worst, was just offensive. The dining room had more of the same, including a ten-foot square painting of a 1940's diner. The rest of it, the master bedroom, the guest bedrooms, gameroom, den, kitchen, and many baths gave you that empty feeling you get when you look at furniture displays in a department store, merchandise that's fighting an uphill battle against a layer of fine dust. All of the knickknacks thrown together like that, they simply reek of evanescence and mortality. That's the way this house was: the jaded, neoclassic fantasies of a dying decorator forever on the make for the glory that was Greece and the grandeur that was Rome.

There were family photos of Freeman with his wife and sons. The wife was a nice number. Her figure had a lean, straight, yet languidly graceful line to it, but her ever-present bright lip gloss hung a sign around a hard, rapacious smile that made a shambles of her perfect dental work. She looked about as tender as a piece of grizzled chuck steak. The boys looked like they were away at college, taking drugs, and having lots of fun.

Making a second trip up to the top floor, I was wasting my time. Then I opened a door I'd missed.

33

She was lovely, like nothing I'd ever seen. Her naked back glowed warmly with a clear, pale blush that one second looked perfectly white, the next slightly pink or purple in its opalescence. In a narrow room lined with showy, gilt-edged leatherbound volumes, she lay on her side, facing away, half-covered by a patchwork quilt, on a long, narrow tan suede couch that would have appeared to belong to an analyst if there had been a chair. It pointed its angled foot at me from the room's short far corner. A standing cranestyled lamp spotted her red hair, turning it a golden cherry color as it fanned out over the pages of an open book. Her head was pillowed there, eyes closed, reading glasses tilted up onto her forehead—she was sound asleep. There was a sherry glass on one of the waist-high shelves at an arm's reach behind.

The drapes were pulled back from the two tall dormer windows. Rivulets of mercurylike water trickled down the one behind the reading light. The other stayed dark. You could see her vertebrae. There was a deep dimple at the base of her spine and her back was wide at the shoulders, creating a streamlining effect which cinched her small waist and blossomed at the hips—a little like a Gibson girl with her hair down.

I stood by the lamp, studied her face, and tried to tally up what I knew about her. A lot and yet not too much: fine young actress, capricious, because otherwise she never would have opened her door to me or, for that matter, listened to my jive line on the phone; passionate and sad in a way that didn't quite make sense. She was a muck of despondency, frustration, and fear. She'd known why but she hadn't told me.

Yeah, it wasn't much. Whatever linked us up, I found it hard to imagine her setting out to deliberately hurt me. But you never know.

I switched the lamp off and on a bit. She opened her eyes and squinted up with a quizzical expression.

"Hi, Susan. Will you be my valentine?"

She latched onto the blanket, covered herself, then turned onto her back and sat up, clasping the quilt to her throat.

"What are you doing here?"

"Funny. I was about to ask you the same question."

She swept off the glasses and dropped them to the floor. Her dark eyes were scorching. "Let's cut the patter," she said with a low, harsh voice.

"Hey, that's fine with me."

She leaned forward and whispered hoarsely, "Gene's crazy."

"Yeah, I know. We met this morning, I think. Seems like a year ago. I'm sure you remember."

"He'll do something. You must *leave.*"

"Nah, sweetie. This is bigger than the both of us."

"Cut it out!"

She put her hand to her mouth too late to quiet the outburst.

"I'm looking for somebody else—bears no resemblance to you whatsoever."

She didn't seem to know what I was talking about. "Please, I don't like this."

"Susan, I'm sorry, but I don't care whether you like it."

The door swung inward and Freeman barged in with Steifer following. He was wearing that smug smile fiercely.

Freeman raised his hands above his head, applauding like a polite courtier, then chimed with fake cheer: "Superb detecting! After ten minutes, you opened the right door. And now that you've had your fun, if you leave immediately, I bet you'll get away."

He took me by the elbow and started to walk me toward the door. I shrugged him off. He turned and sprang at me like a crazed alley cat, gouging at my face with all his nails. Steifer jumped him, but not before I tapped some Morse code upside his head, culminating with a Sunday punch that split my knuckles.

Steifer let go of him, frowned, and backed out into the hall. Freeman slumped back against the bookcase, then slid the rest of the way to the floor. A moment later, Steifer was back with a glass of water. Susan and I were staring at each other. I watched as Steifer patted Freeman's cheeks and threw the water in his face.

"I think she set me up," I told Steifer.

"What is this?" Susan demanded.

Steifer ignored her. "How do you mean?" he asked me.

"They found out I was onto his dead brother."

"You're mad!" she screamed. "Who are you?!" she demanded, turning to Steifer.

"Police."

"What has any of this to do with you?"

"A lot."

I pointed at Freeman. He was shaking his head and groaning. "This man murdered his brother, for what reason I don't know and I don't care."

"Crap!" Freeman shouted."Try me with crap. They told me he's missing. Don't pretend I'm happy about it."

"I'd venture to say it's a combination of brotherly hate and self-interest. He's big in construction, probably around Hollywood. Well, him and a million other guys stood to be hurt by what his Councilman brother wanted to do there."

"Which was what?" asked Susan.

"Basically, he wanted to pass an ordinance so that all adult entertainment would be centered in Hollywood—to keep the rest of the city clean."

Freeman was wobbly getting to his feet. He wasn't smug anymore. His wet beard was flat and stringy; underneath that, his jaw was out of whack. He winced and massaged it as he talked. "Don' say anything, darling," he admonished. "These guys are crazy. They have absolutely no idea what they're talking about, and I'm going to put them in jail."

He walked over to Susan, sat down, and put his arm around her. "Don't let them confuse you," he told her in a confidential tone.

"Listen," I continued, "your loverboy's another story. He's this man's concern," I said, nodding toward Steifer. "I got this boy, my son, somebody took him and I gotta find him. Gene here or one of his fingermen knocked off the guys who took him—understand me?"

She shook her head. "No. What's the relationship?"

"These guys—the ones who were killed—they found Gene's brother's body. They didn't know who he was, but that's beside the point. Councilman Freeman was supposed to quietly disappear. If murder was suspected, there was the danger of publicity, and you never know where that might lead. This initiative the Councilman was pushing might have gathered steam all by itself."

"And these kidnappers, you think Gene murdered them because they found his brother whom Gene also murdered?"

"You're crazy!" the man yelled at me. "Crazy!" He shook Susan. "I told you: *don't say anything*. Don't you see? They'll twist what we say."

Steifer elbowed me out of the way and yanked Freeman off the couch.

"One thing is all I care about," I said to her. "Do you know anything?"

"Haven't they insulted us enough?" wailed Freeman.

"Do you know anything?"

"Don't listen to him! Look at me."

Susan looked at the man.

"That's better." His smug smile strained for a comeback. "Snookums, it's me," he said, patting his chest. "Homicidal maniac, yes or no? It's absurd, darling," he gestured toward her with both arms outspread.

"I—" she started.

"Honey," he butted in, "I know that look. Let's not air our dirty laundry, please."

"Gene, but I don't know about your business."

"Can it!!"

"You get what you want, don't you?"

"Don't you?"

She turned to me, smiling bitterly. "Normally, he's not that bad of a guy. It's tempting when a man comes along. He worships you and has no idea what to do with his big money. What do you do?"

"That's your problem," I said.

"It's not a problem. It's a delight, an *adventure*," she said throatily. She held the quilt, scooted down and touched my arm. "This is silly, you won't believe me, but you have no idea how expert they are at making bruises that don't show."

Freeman was talking to Steifer in a husky, whiney voice. "She's incoherent. Can't you see she's under treatment? Don't listen to her."

"Sure."

She gave Freeman a mock salute. Her eyes gleamed brightly, went a little wide. "Yes, sir," she said. "Listen to the man."

"Susan, do you know anything?"

"I wish I did," she said throatily, without the sarcasm.

"Did you see a thirteen-year-old boy, small, long blond hair, dressed up in cowboy clothes?"

"No."

"Hear Gene or anybody say anything that might have anything to do with it?" Steifer asked.

I kicked out at a shelf, then I turned to Steifer. "I'm all fucked up," I told him. "Is she leveling?"

He gave me a nod.

"Well, then," I said to her. "Now we know each other's stories."

34

Steifer walked me to the door. He wasn't sure what he was going to do. He wanted to haul Freeman in, but he didn't have anything on him. There was nothing so far, it seemed, linking him to the Councilman's murder; and, for all we knew, the Councilman hadn't even been murdered. Sure, his body had skipped town and a number of interested bystanders were no longer standing by, but Gardena had his remains, along with the autopsy report, and so far they'd been stonewalling on their information. We had to work fast on opening things up. The dead hit man was waiting for an ID in that ranch house out in Chatsworth, and affidavits had to be gotten from the Councilman's wife, family, and associates.

George had made some phone calls. One of his men was coming over to pick him up. He handed me his keys and gave me directions back to his BMW, and was wondering aloud whether it was going to be safe for the lady when she appeared on the stairs. She was wearing her heavy blue gray overcoat buttoned up over faded jeans. Her feet were in a pair of Dutch clogs. Her eyes were puffy and her face looked too pale. Steifer turned toward her.

"Can one of you give me a ride?" she said.

"I was just leaving," I told her.

Steifer lifted a finger at her. "One minute, OK?"

Then he pulled me into the dining room. I knew what he was going to say before he said it. His mouth had a stoic set to it. He laid his hands on my shoulders, but when he looked at me he took them away. He gave me a tight-lipped little smile.

"OK, I won't give you a pep talk . . . but don't give up. I've seen these turn out rotten, but you just never know, Ben, I'm tellin' you—anything can happen."

"Yeah."

"I got a hunch. I can smell it—we're gonna find him."

"You're a good guy, George," was all I could say.

"Well, if you weren't such a likable *schmuck*, why would I care?" he frowned.

"From the first time we tangoed, who would have thought we'd ever waltz together?"

He laughed too much at this, and slapped me on the arm. "That's better."

I was glad he thought so.

35

We said nothing on the way to the car. Barefoot, she walked before or behind me, carrying the wooden shoes in one hand. Stanley fussed over her once we got in, then he curled up on the back seat. We drove to her place in silence. She smoked. I put the radio on once or twice and pushed all the buttons out of curiosity. Steifer listened to rock, country-western, and classical. When I pulled up, she told me she was sorry about my son and hoped I would find him. I thanked her for her sentiments and drove away, trying not to think about her.

I wasn't satisfied with what I'd seen of the house where we'd found Aikens' partner. There wasn't much point to it, but I had to check it out again. The downpour was running out on itself, going hard, then slowing to a heavy drizzle every few minutes. I found my way over in about ten minutes. Two black-and-whites were in the driveway, three were in the street. It looked like a party —of cops. I saw a pair in the dining room window. Steifer had called it in. I drove past, turned around, and parked in front. When I opened the car door, Stanley jumped out to take a leak. He kept jouncing away, so I left him under a jungle of camellia bushes and headed for the front door.

A cop was coming down the center front hall. His hand was down by his side. He was ready to draw on me, which gave me some idea of what I must have looked like.

I put my hands up. Lights came from behind as the coroner's wagon pulled in and parked at the end of the driveway.

"What's up?" he asked casually.

"I was here with George Steifer about forty-five minutes ago," I explained. "I'd like to take another look around."

"What are you looking for?"

"He's the guy with the kid," somebody said from out of range.

I let my hands down. Armstead, Steifer's partner from the La Brea Tar Pits, came into view and waved me forward.

"He's OK. Come on in, Mister Crandel."

I walked in the house. The gunslinger walked away. Armstead wanted to shake hands.

"Sorry about your troubles," he said. "Right this way."

He escorted me into the dining room. Al Butera was where we'd left him and there were five guys in uniform standing around the table. You would have thought it was a wake. Armstead told them who I was and said I wanted to look around. The only one without muddy feet, a burly, boyish-looking lieutenant, chomped the fat cigar below his moustache and Shirley Temple hair, stared me down, and said he was sorry but they couldn't have that. Then he told two of the boys to go check their radio, got down on his knees, and started running his hand over the carpet. The two cops who were left followed his example. Armstead jerked his head toward the hall and we walked out.

"Good luck. We're doing all we can," the lieutenant muttered around his cigar.

"We put a flash under the foundation, checked everything," Armstead was saying.

Stanley was howling. I walked toward the rear of the house and looked out the kitchen window. Armstead stayed right by my side.

"That's your dog," he said warmly.

I stood there watching Stanley and looking over the backyard.

Armstead saw me looking toward the garage. "Nothing in there—in case you were wondering. We checked already."

Stanley was sniffing around the shuffleboard court.

"Look at him," I said.

"It's the rain," Armstead said. "They go crazy when they begin to lose their scent. I got a beagle, Snoopy," Armstead smiled to himself.

"He wasn't doing that before."

Armstead turned to me with concern creasing his brow. "He's gonna catch cold."

"Yeah."

We went out the back door just in time to meet a honey of a downpour. Armstead hung back against the rear of the house. There was lightning and a long peal of thunder that came off like a sound engineer was monkeying around recording somebody peeling back the lid on a sardine tin.

"Shit, look at that," sighed Armstead.

I bent down to pick up Stanley. He was standing at the edge of the shuffleboard, digging into the muddy, over-grown grass. He planted himself as I tried to get him up, then he snarled at me. I let go. He moved away and kept sniffing; then he came back, walked about, and sniffed some more. He stood on the smooth wet cement, growled, looked up into the downpour and howled like there was no tomorrow.

"Stanley!"

I went after him. He slid away from me, I slipped and fell backwards. My hands shot out to break the fall and, as I came down, I felt something give, very slightly. The shuffleboard was cement, but it had been poured into a mold set on top of the ground, not flush into it as most are. There was a two-inch ridge that had been camou-flaged by the fringe of grass. I gripped it and tried to lift. Armstead came out and asked me what I was doing. There was a metallic sound. The thing was on a metal base. I leaned into the lift and it slid forward a touch. I pushed it. It moved the entire length of the court. Arm-stead knelt down and worked with me. We pushed the lid off and skinned our wet shins over a damp but dry, rough cement ground.

"It's one of those bomb shelters," marvelled Armstead.

The rain drummed upon a metal hatch at the left end. Drumming was coming from inside it. I rushed over and pulled on a recessed handle. It came up.

He was there, all of him, all in one piece. His eyes shined in the dark. He was standing on a small step lad-der. I pulled him out of the ground.

"Dad," he said.

36

He wanted Chinese food. Over the next few days, we had lots of it, along with chili dogs, banana splits, pizza with everything on it. You name it, we had it; and you can bet your shirt that Stanley got his full share. I consumed enough starch to run a laundry and put on five pounds. When the weather cleared, we went day fishing beyond Malibu at Paradise Cove. We passed by Sam's. She'd been very understanding; after all, she'd said, bucks were "nothing to get all bent out of shape over." It's too bad Aikens, Al, Freeman, and company hadn't seen it her way. Rich people really are different. Some of them actually believe they aren't dependent upon money. It seems to come easy to them because they'll do just about anything to get it. Whatever, my money bag had kept company with Petey underground, I'd turned it over to Sam, and she was supposed to be trying to work something out. She'll probably file an insurance claim and parlay the hot cash into a small fortune; meanwhile, I've got a fifty-thousand-dollar monkey on my back.

Win a few, lose a few. Anyway, after things settled down, I wanted to see Susan Grady. It was about a week later when I called her. She sounded glad to hear from me. Matter-of-factly, she told me that Freeman was in trouble. His wife, back fresh from a European holiday, had decided that she had taken all she could stand. As the saying goes, you could write a book: Freeman was into this, into that. He had all the connections, but he was slick and slippery and there was no doubt he'd get away.

Susan said that she and Mrs. Freeman had police protection until the prelims were over. She wasn't looking forward to it. I finally got up my nerve to change the subject. I asked if I could see her for dinner. She was starting a play, there were rehearsals every night, so we settled on cocktails somewhere close by.

That afternoon, before lunch, I got a twenty-five dollar haircut at a place where they gave you a before-and-after shampoo and condition and called the barbers "hair designers." After lunch, I put a three-hundred-dollar suit on my MasterCharge. It was a smooth classic charcoal gray flannel with narrow lapels. I bought a tie and shoes to go with it. On the way home, I stopped and bought a white silk display handkerchief. I cut myself shaving, but after I got assembled, I felt confident I was worthy of a double take from a sympathetic eye.

I was ready. I caught a double bill to kill time, then I picked up a mixed bouquet of white and red roses and went over there. A plainclothes team was parked in front. The one in the back seat rolled down his streetside window.

"Excuse me, sir."

I went over and handed him my license. He looked at me, looked at my license, sucked a tooth, and rolled his tongue around his gums. His face was oily, his collar open. His partner was the same way, only fatter, with his feet up on the front seat. Styrofoam cups and food containers were piled up around them. They'd been sitting for awhile.

When he gave the license back, he looked me over, smiled broadly, and said, "She's expecting you."

I felt like I was wearing my first pair of trousers. The rotund driver had a bloated face with a short, hooked nose and no chin. He belched sotto voce and gave me a mischievous leer with a one-two wink and twinkle.

"Have a good time," he said.

I smiled like an altar boy, walked up to the door, turned around, and looked back to see if they were looking over my shoulder. Their car was curtained over with the shadow of a curbside tree under the streetlight.

I rang and squeezed the flowers. My hands were clammy by the time I heard her on the stairs. She opened the door wearing a red, fuchsia, lavender orchid print dress with a head band of the same material. Her stockings were lavender; the open-toed high heels were bright red. She had a black sweater and matching beaded bag under one arm. The color set her hair on fire and she had this huge girlish smile that, for some reason, once she looked at me, disappeared into thin air.

I handed her the bouquet. "For you," I said.

She took them with a smile that was going rickety at the edges. "Thank you," she said. "You're very sweet."

"What's wrong?"

She shook her head and looked down.

I stood there, trying to shrug off what was hitting me. I put my finger under her chin, lifted it, and stared into a pair of black violet eyes I'd never seen before. I was like a moth before the light. Everything in me wanted to take hold of her and press her to me, but I held back. I told her she was beautiful. She nodded as the tears started down her face. Then she curled into my arms and held me like a big teddy bear. I smoothed her hair.

"You want a lot, don't you?" she said.

"Well, yeah," I admitted.

She let go and stood back. "I didn't realize you expected so much."

"I don't *expect* anything," I told her. "I was just hoping that you'd—"

"It's not the right time for me," she said stubbornly.

"But—"

"This would lead too quickly to—you know—something permanent, and I can't handle that right now."

I put my hands in my pockets and tilted back and forth on my heels. Quickly, she reached up, flung her arms around my neck, and put a send-off on me I'll never forget. It was as if I'd swallowed a fuse box that went down my throat and sprouted sparks from my toes. When she let go, I had to swallow to catch my breath.

"L.A.'s such a small town," she said.

"Yeah," I agreed. "That's what I hate about it."

"We're just going to have to run into each other. By then, we'll be ready. We'll start over. We'll have a real courtship, take it nice and slow—you know—like they used to."

She clapped her hands together, looking like a little girl who'd just received a record number of valentines.

That's when we'd met, two days before Valentine's Day. I should have thought of that—being premature and all—because the next time I did run into her it was a few weeks later and she was with another man. He looked like me—with a smile. We stopped, chatted, ordered fast-food together, then went our separate ways. I like to think the veiled look she gave me was one of epic, forlorn tragedy. Maybe it was—who knows?

That night, Petey and I had dinner at home. I should say he ate, I was on a liquid protein diet of the ninety proof variety. After we were done, Petey pushed his plate aside and took a crumpled pack of Kools out of his pocket.

"Don't smoke," I told him. "It's shitty for your health."

He smiled, jerked his head at my bottle, and lit up.

"My man, my man," I said. "Look at me. Look me in the eyes."

He planted his elbows over the table, leaned across, and stuck his face in mine, holding back the big guffaw.

I didn't flinch. When I started talking, he drew back from my breath. "That's right, big shot," I told him. "Dear old dad has an A 1 buzz on. He's going out tonight and he's going to get into a little trouble—not much, just a little . . . cleanse out the system . . . year-end inventory—some day I'll tell you about it. But—" and I raised a declamatory finger at this juncture—"please remember: Just because I don't set that good an example *do not* mean I don't know what's good for ya once in a while—got me, kid?"

He smoked like a goddamn chimney, smirked, and looked very, very bored.

"I want you to be better than me, happier an' everything. And you're gonna be 'cause you got better opportunities. Me, like everybody else, I got problems, I am no ideal parent, but I'm all you got. *I* understand you."

"No, you don't."

"Well, nobody understands *anybody* completely. But I try . . . so you do, too, OK?"

No answer.

"Now, Petey, *please put out that cigarette!*"

"And *you* take a cab."

"Shake."